DANNY DANGER

and the
SPACE TWISTER

ADAM FROST

nosy
crow

To Isabel, Kyle and Aliana

First published in the UK in 2012 by Nosy Crow Ltd
The Crow's Nest, 10a Lant Street
London, SE1 1QR, UK

Nosy Crow and associated logos are trademarks and/or
registered trademarks of Nosy Crow Ltd

Text © Adam Frost, 2012
Illustrations © Andy Parker, 2012

A CIP catalogue record for this book is available from the British Library

Printed and bound in the UK by
Clays Ltd, St Ives Plc

Papers used by Nosy Crow are made from wood grown in sustainable forests.

ISBN: 978 0 857 63029 2

www.nosycrow.com

1
OPEN

Danny Danger walked down his local high street with his cosmic remote held tightly in his hand. He looked at the time on its display: 08:55. The shops wouldn't open for five minutes and he couldn't face the wait. He slipped into a doorway, where nobody would notice him, and jammed his thumb down on Fast Forward.

Everything and everyone in the street sped up. An old lady in a mobility vehicle whizzed by like she was in the Grand Prix; two tubby businessmen zipped past like they were Olympic sprinters; a man walking a dog shot across the road, as if the dog had just seen a squirrel.

In shop windows, Closed signs were instantly

flipped to Open; lights came on; doors sprung open; tables and boxes appeared on the pavement that were full of fruit, vegetables, flowers, fish, lightbulbs, saucepans, newspapers and books.

Danny pressed Pause. Everyone in the street became a statue, frozen in time and space. A small boy on a skateboard had jumped over a pothole and was now suspended in mid-air with a grin on his face. Two delivery men were halfway across the pavement, carrying a giant fridge out of a shop, their faces screwed up with the effort. Danny almost wanted to press Play again so they could put the fridge down.

But first he had to go shopping.

Danny looked down at the cosmic remote

before he put it back in his pocket, smiling at the chunky buttons: Record, Play, Stop, Pause, Rewind, Fast Forward, On/Off, and the amber crystal embedded in its back that made it work. It really had been the most incredible birthday present ever. He smiled again, slipped it into his pocket, and headed for the bookshop.

The funny thing was that, until that morning, Danny hadn't used his remote for weeks.

He had used it a lot when his uncle Charlie had first given it to him but that was mostly because his parents had tried to throw all his possessions away, he'd been kidnapped by a robot parrot and an evil genius called the Night Scientist had tried to kill him, Uncle Charlie, his big sister, Mia, and his best friend, Eric. The cosmic remote had been his only weapon.

But, since then, life had got better. For a start, Uncle Charlie had come to stay for a few weeks which meant that his demented parents couldn't tell him off, or bully him, or kick him out. Then there was Mia, who had used to be demented too but who was now completely on his side, defending him and shielding him when his parents were on the warpath. Best of all, his closest friend Eric had a brand-new ZONGA megadrive, which had all the latest 3D games on it, and which Eric's mum let them play for ninety whole minutes every evening.

But that morning had not been a good morning. Without his remote, it would have been even worse.

It had started when his father had waddled sideways into his room, with a big black bag of rubbish between his legs. His mother had followed his father.

"Good morning, Daniel," said Mrs Danger, looking down her long beak of a nose. "As you know, the council have a new rule where we're only allowed to put out two rubbish bags a week. What an absolute disgrace! I fill three bags a week with used J-cloths alone. I fail to see how anyone in the street can keep their house clean in such circumstances, especially if they have children bringing in dirt and germs and nasty smells the whole day."

"Smells," grunted Mr Danger, putting the rubbish bag down at the foot of Danny's bed.

Mrs Danger pulled out a rag and started to polish the handle of Danny's bedroom door, talking at the same time. "Still, your father and I have thought of a way round this. Haven't we, Hector?"

"Way round," said Mr Danger.

"Since you live in complete filth and squalor all the time without even blinking an eyelid, we thought you wouldn't mind if we used your room for any excess rubbish."

"Rubbish!" thundered Mr Danger, waggling a fat finger at Danny.

"We've got about twenty bags downstairs," said Mrs Danger, "and that's just from yesterday."

Danny stared at his mother in anger and disbelief.

"You might want to open your bedroom window for the first time in your entire life," said his mother with a crooked smile. She put the rag back in her pocket and turned to leave.

Danny watched his mother walk across the landing, past one of the framed tea towels that she had put up everywhere in the house. They all had a similar message: clean everything, all the time. This one read:

> **RUB AND SCRUB WITH STRENGTH AND SPEED UNTIL YOUR FINGERS START TO BLEED.**

Danny found the remote in his pocket and pressed Pause.

It felt odd because for the last two months, whenever Danny's mother had pulled a stunt like this, either his uncle or his sister had been standing in front of him, daring them to take it further. His uncle had left a week ago, returning to his work as a EUREKA! agent and protecting the world from evil inventors. But where was Mia?

He looked at Mia's bedroom door and then across at the frozen form of his mother. He had to deal with his parents first.

He squeezed past them on the stairs, ran through the kitchen and opened the back door, staring at where the rubbish bags were piled up. He carefully made a small tear in each of them, then went back upstairs and positioned himself in the doorway of his room. He pressed Play.

"Fair enough," he said.

"What?" said Mrs Danger.

"That sounds fair enough," repeated Danny. "Not on the bed, but anywhere else is fine."

"For heaven's sake, Hector!" huffed Mrs Danger. "This was supposed to be a punishment but it's more like a reward."

The first bag split halfway up the stairs, sending tin cans bouncing down into the hall.

"You fool, Hector!" exclaimed Mrs Danger. "Oh, just leave it there, I'll sort it out. You get the next one."

The tear that Danny had made in the second bag was much smaller, so the pressure of the rubbish kept anything from falling out until the landing, where a seeping paper bag full of rotten vegetables plopped out. "Did you double bag it, Hector?" hissed Mrs Danger. "Get the next one!"

The third and fourth bags split in the kitchen. The fifth bag exploded as Mr Danger was coming through the back door, covering him in grass clippings and weedkiller.

By the time Danny crossed the landing to knock on Mia's door, the stairs were a solid slide of junk, the hall was like a municipal tip and the stench from the kitchen was so strong that the wallpaper everywhere seemed to be rippling and peeling off.

Danny could hear his mother wailing in the living room, clutching fistfuls of rubbish in her bare hands.

"Mia," said Danny, knocking on her door. "You've got to see this."

There was no answer, so Danny opened the door. Mia was sitting on the edge of her bed.

"You OK?" asked Danny.

"Yeah," said Mia. "Yeah, I'm OK."

"What's happened?" asked Danny.

"Nothing," said Mia. "Seriously, there's nothing wrong."

"But—" began Danny.

"It's my birthday, that's all," said Mia. "April the third."

"Oh, no, I—"

"Mum and Dad didn't even mention it," said his sister. "I mean, they always give me awful presents so I suppose it doesn't matter. But I thought maybe this year... Uncle Charlie might, you know. And Eric and me get along pretty well now – and..."

Mia's face snapped back to its usual self-possessed state. "Forget about it. It's fine. Birthdays are for little kids. It's just a day, isn't it? It's just a Saturday."

Danny pressed Pause.

He couldn't believe he'd forgotten his sister's birthday. He couldn't believe he'd been so stupid and so self-absorbed. Part of the problem was that, last year, Mia and he had been sworn enemies, so he had no reason to remember her birthday. But now it was different. Mia had chosen to take on his parents and stick up for him. So if he didn't remember her birthday, who would?

He looked at the time on the remote: *10:33*. He pressed Rewind and the orange crystal on the back of the remote spun round. Mia whizzed round her room, reading magazines backwards, putting clothes back in her wardrobe, and climbing back into bed.

It was *08:23*. Danny pressed Stop.

He walked on to the landing. His parents weren't awake yet either. He could go to the high street, choose something nice for Mia and bring it home in time for breakfast.

So here he was, the remote back in his pocket, diving into the bookshop, then the clothes shop, then the music shop. He looked at a kitten in the pet shop and a Venus fly trap in the florist. He went into the newsagent's and tried to remember the magazines that Mia liked reading.

When he came out, he looked at the time on his remote: *09:11*. He needed a bit longer. He wanted Mia to have her present as soon as she woke up, so he pressed Pause.

Everyone in the street froze again. He walked back towards the bookshop. There was a new Minty Squelcher novel out and Mia had all the other books in the series. He'd buy her that and perhaps a poster of her favourite band.

As he crossed a side street, he noticed a young man sitting on a bench opposite the florist's. He seemed to be staring straight at Danny. He had long dark hair, a pinstripe suit and shiny black shoes. His eyes were two different colours – one brown, one blue. His mouth was slightly open and Danny could see diamonds, rubies and other jewels shining in his teeth. Most strikingly of all, he had a long scar down the middle of his face, starting in the centre of his forehead, cutting his nose in two and running down on to his chin and neck.

Danny was pretty sure he'd never seen the man in his town before. And the oddest thing was that, even though Danny had paused the world, the man seemed to be breathing; the man seemed to be blinking.

He couldn't be. It wasn't possible.

Danny went into the bookshop. He found the book he wanted and left the right money on the counter. The thought of the man with the scar still made him uneasy. But worse was to come. When he opened the door of the bookshop, the man with the scar had gone.

The man couldn't have moved, not unless Danny had picked him up and moved him. Danny felt his chest pounding, his legs growing weak.

Then he glanced up the street and saw a young couple holding hands. The man was pointing at a shop window; the woman was halfway through a laugh. In between them, Danny saw the man with the scar. The man was frozen too – not moving, not flinching. But Danny swore he could see the man's breath rising in clouds in the cold morning air.

It was time to go. Mia would understand. He'd got her the book; the poster could wait.

Danny looked back up at the man with the scar. The man hadn't moved or changed his expression. Perhaps Danny had accidentally pressed Play for a few seconds while he was in the bookshop, when he had been fumbling for his money.

That was it! Of course that was it! That was the only explanation that made sense. Danny had jumped to all the wrong conclusions. The man wasn't immune from the remote. Nobody was – except Danny.

He'd buy Mia the poster after all. He went into the newsagent's again, found a suitable poster, and left the right money on the counter. This time, he kept his remote in his hand. He kept his fingers away from the buttons.

He came back outside, the poster under one arm and the book under the other. He looked up the street and saw the young couple holding hands. The man with the scar wasn't there.

Danny ran. He dropped the book; he dropped the poster. He ran back down the high street, weaving round the frozen people, not looking back, running faster and faster.

The man with the scar stepped out from

behind a tree and put his foot out. Danny tripped over it, but kept his balance. He staggered forward, flung his arms out and kept running.

"These shoes aren't exactly built for speed," sighed the man with the scar, "but needs must."

He calmly tied up the laces on his right shoe and then sprinted after Danny.

The next two minutes were a *blur.*

Danny had a vague memory of being bundled to the ground, something being rolled over his thumb, someone going through his pockets and snipping off a lock of his hair.

When he came round, he found himself lying on the ground outside the off-licence. A policeman was leaning over him saying, "You can't sleep there, son. Run along now."

Danny felt his pockets. The remote was gone. His right thumb was covered with something green and sticky. He couldn't believe he'd lost the remote for the second time in his life.

"I won't tell you again, you spotty Herbert," said the policeman. "Sling your hook."

"I'm going, I'm going," said Danny.

Danny walked back down the high street, trying to understand what had happened. He had paused the world; he had stopped time. Perhaps the man with the scar had a remote too. But if so, why did he need Danny's?

Nothing made sense. Everything felt wrong.

Danny wanted to crawl into a bin and curl up into a ball. That reminded him that his parents would be filling his room with rubbish about now. Without his remote, he'd just have to let them do it. That was one reason he didn't want to go home. The other was Mia. He had forgotten her birthday, so to put it right, he had used his cosmic remote, only someone had seen it and stolen it. Now it was gone: never to be found, never to be returned.

She'd take that badly.

Danny turned down the side street that led back to his house. On the corner, there was an electrical shop with rows of TVs in the window. He noticed that people were gathering in front of the TVs and chatting loudly. Danny was curious and joined them.

Usually the TVs showed different types of programmes – films, soap operas, music videos – but today they were all tuned to news channels. On one TV, a reporter was interviewing a policewoman outside a large grey building. The ticker at the bottom of the screen read:

£10 BILLION GONE FROM LONDON BANK

On another screen, there was footage of an army base and a headline reading:

SEVEN LUXURY YACHTS VANISH

On the biggest screen, there was a shot of a few large houses surrounded by palm trees with the headline:

POPULATION OF CARIBBEAN ISLAND DISAPPEAR

"It must be aliens, mustn't it?" one old lady was saying.

"It's probably just kids messing about," said

a middle-aged man with big glasses.

"I think it's pirates," said one young woman, "or witches. Or the Mafia. Or computer hackers."

Danny couldn't hear them. He was staring at one of the TV screens, not really looking at it, just gazing at something or someone behind it. He knew what was happening. He knew who was doing this.

He looked down at the sticky glue on his thumb. When he'd first got the remote, Uncle Charlie had made sure that no one else but Danny could use it. If it wasn't Danny's thumb pressing the buttons, then it wouldn't work. The man with the scar must have taken Danny's fingerprints. Which meant that the man with the scar would be able to use the remote.

Danny looked at the TV screens again. This was his fault. And surely this was just the beginning.

"Hello, Danny," said a voice behind him. "How come you're watching telly in the street like an old person?"

Danny turned round. It was his best friend, Eric.

"Eric, look at the news," said Danny. "I did this. Me."

Another story had flashed up on the biggest screen:

CAGES LEFT OPEN IN BRISTOL ZOO

There was footage of a monkey throwing doughnuts at a nun.

"That's you in a monkey suit?" asked Eric.

At that moment, Eric's mum appeared behind them.

"We should go back home in a minute, Eric, love," she said. "Lots of strange things seem to be happening. I just saw Mrs Billabong and she says people have been told to stay indoors."

"OK, I'll catch up with you," said Eric to his mum. Then he turned back to Danny. "So what were you saying? And try not to sound bonkers this time."

Danny explained what had happened that morning – his sister's forgotten birthday, going to the shops, the man with the scar, losing his remote.

Eric was staring at the TV screens now. The latest story was:

BUCKINGHAM PALACE SUDDENLY PAINTED GREEN

"So he's just pressing Pause and Rewind and Fast Forward and doing whatever he wants?" asked Eric.

Danny nodded.

They both spoke at the same time. "What are we going to do?"

"Eric, come on," called his mum. "It's dangerous out here."

"Coming!" shouted Eric.

"What CAN we do?" said Danny. "He's got the remote. And it's different from last time, cos he's got it to work straightaway."

"What about EUREKA!" said Eric. "And your uncle Charlie?"

"Uncle Charlie calls every week to check on me," said Danny, "but he calls me on the remote."

"Oh," said Eric. "Bum."

A split second later, Mia was standing in front of them.

"There you are, Danny," she said. "You've got to get home. You know, Dad's been heaping up rubbish in your room. It's like the back of a dustcart in there. You'll have to use your remote."

"I know but—" began Danny.

"And another thing, where's my birthday present?" said his sister.

"That's what—" stammered Danny.

"You too," said Mia, pointing at Eric. "Where's my present?"

"I – er—" began Eric.

"I haven't had one single ruddy present!" said Mia. "What's the matter with me? Do I smell? Do I have scary eyes? An annoying laugh? A screechy voice?"

"Well, yeah," said Eric, "but that's not why we didn't get you a present."

Before Mia could grab Eric by the throat, Danny explained everything. "You're angry, aren't you?" he said at the end.

"Of course I'm angry," said Mia.

"I knew you'd be angry," said Danny.

"What did you expect me to be? Pleased? Bored? Not fussed one way or the other? Last time you lost the remote, you nearly got yourself – and the rest of us – killed."

"Well, if it hadn't been your stupid birthday, I'd never have left the house in the first place!" shouted Danny.

"You could have just remembered like a normal person and got me a present the day before!"

Eric's mother appeared again. "Oh hello, you two," she said to Danny and Mia. "Listen, Eric, we've got to get inside. Something's gone very wrong with the world. If you want Mia and Danny to come with you, that's fine. But we've got to go. Now."

Eric, Danny and Mia were suddenly aware of everyone else on the high street getting into cars or walking quickly back to their houses. Shopkeepers were speedily winding up awnings and pulling down shutters. It was as if they were fast forwarding time all by themselves.

Danny, Eric and Mia walked back to Eric's house in silence, all of them brooding, all of them trying to work out what to do.

Eric's mother left them in Eric's room, saying, "Don't move until I work out what's going on."

She closed the bedroom door. For a few seconds, Eric, Danny and Mia remained silent. Then Danny and Mia started talking at once.

"I don't understand how this man with a scar wasn't affected by the remote," said Mia.

"Why didn't Uncle Charlie warn me? Why didn't Uncle Charlie stop him?" said Danny.

Eric was peering out the window.

"The fun's not over yet," he said. "Take a look at Mrs Macready's front garden."

Danny and Mia came to the window. They looked at the house next to theirs. In the front garden, instead of the silver-haired old lady that lived there, they saw a huge man in dark glasses silently trimming the hedge.

"There too!" whispered Mia.

They looked at the house on the other side of theirs. Instead of Mr or Mrs Singh, they saw another huge man in dark glasses, also trimming the hedge.

"I don't get it," said Danny. "What are they doing there?"

"Well, they're not gardeners," said Eric. "That one on the left is holding the shears upside down."

"But I haven't got the remote any more," said Danny. "And if the man with the scar wanted to finish me off, why didn't he do it when he took the remote?"

Both of the men stopped trimming the hedge and stared up the street.

"I think I get it," said Mia.

A postman was walking along the pavement with a parcel under his arm.

"Look at the package, Danny," said Mia.

Danny squinted at the parcel and saw that it was covered with stamps of all shapes, colours and sizes. He started thinking. Uncle Charlie had originally sent Danny his cosmic remote in a parcel like that. Uncle Charlie worked for an organisation called EUREKA! that looked after incredible inventions. He travelled the world, making sure that new gadgets didn't fall into the hands of bad people. Sometimes EUREKA! loaned these gadgets out to people who really needed them. Danny, with his rotten parents and awful teacher, had needed the cosmic remote to rewind and pause and fast forward his way out of trouble.

So, Danny thought, what could Uncle Charlie be sending him now? What Danny needed – what he needed more than ever – was his cosmic remote. But that was gone; that couldn't be in the box.

Danny was brought back to the present by a nudge from Mia. The two men were putting their shears down and stepping on to the pavement. They walked up to the postman and stood either side of him. There was a scuffle which ended with the postman being thrown into Mrs Macready's hedge.

One of the huge men was now holding the parcel. He dropped it on the floor and stamped on it several times, until it was nothing but wires and brown dust. Then, for some reason, he looked over at Eric's house.

Eric, Danny and Mia ducked down behind the window ledge.

"He saw us, he saw us, he saw us," muttered Eric.

A few seconds passed and Mia put her head up. The two huge men were walking off down the street. She said, "They're going," and slumped back down again. Then she turned to Danny. "So Uncle Charlie must have sent you another gadget. He knows the remote's been stolen."

"Shame those men just smashed it up," said Eric. "I wonder what it was. Maybe a laser gun?

Or a teleporter? Or a mind-control helmet?"

Danny was thinking. He looked up at Mia and Eric and said quietly, "We must have beaten the man with the scar."

"What do you mean?" asked Mia.

"We must have used whatever was in that box to beat him. Or almost beat him," said Danny.

"How do you work that out?" asked Mia.

"Think about it. How would he know that Uncle Charlie was sending me a gadget? And why would he care?"

Mia frowned and shook her head. "You've lost me."

"In the future, we must have used that gadget. We must have used it in a battle with the man with the scar. And he must have stopped us in the nick of time. Then he pressed Rewind to make sure we never got the gadget in the first place."

"Blimey, yeah," said Eric. "So he rewinds time to this exact point to intercept the parcel on its way to your house and sends those men to destroy it. To make sure you never open it." Eric paused and then added, "I wonder how much time he had to rewind. I wonder what we did."

Mia was looking out of the window and thinking.

"So you're saying we've beaten this guy once already," she said.

Danny nodded. "In a future that doesn't exist any more."

"And now we have to beat him again," said Mia.

Danny nodded. "In this future."

"Only this time round we haven't got the amazing gadget?"

Danny nodded. "Now we've got absolutely nothing."

"Well," said Mia flatly, "this is turning out to be a truly excellent birthday."

2
EXIT

Half an hour had passed, and Danny, Mia and Eric were still sitting in Eric's bedroom, not saying much, not doing much – just thinking.

"I wonder what he's doing with the remote now," said Eric. "Maybe we should go downstairs and watch the news?"

"Can't you get the internet on that?" asked Mia, pointing at a box and a monitor.

"No, that's a ZOMBA megadrive," said Eric. "It's just for games. The computer's downstairs."

"For heaven's sake," sighed Mia. "Why can't you just have one computer? That does everything?"

"Well," said Eric. "It's all about different

chipsets doing different jobs. With a console, you want the graphics card to be—"

"All right, all right!" exclaimed Mia. "I don't actually want to know!"

"If we could work out how he did it," said Danny, "if we could make ourselves immune from the remote too, then we'd have a chance of beating him."

"Brilliant!" said Mia. "We should be able to work that out in about – er – fifty years."

Danny was about to reply when there was a knock at the window. They all turned round and saw Danny and Mia's uncle smiling at them. He was hanging from a luminous white cable.

"Uncle Charlie!" cried Mia and Danny.

Eric ran over and hitched up the window.

Uncle Charlie put one foot on the windowsill and then swung himself into the room. The cable vanished and he slipped two small white objects into his pocket.

"I thought I'd find you here," he said. "Nice room, Eric. Is that a ZOMBA megadrive?"

The children all started talking at once.

"How did he take my remote?" asked Danny.

"What was in the parcel?" asked Mia.

"Yeah, it's the ten gigabyte version with wireless controllers," said Eric.

"OK, OK, look," said Uncle Charlie. "Let me tell you what I know. Then ask me any questions at the end."

Danny nodded. Mia pursed her lips.

"Danny's remote was stolen by the Space Twister," began Uncle Charlie. He pulled a photo out of his pocket and showed it to them. "Six feet tall. Twenty-nine years old. Usually well dressed. Nasty temper. Strange sense of humour."

Danny recognised the long dark hair, the scar down the middle of the face and the jewels glinting in the teeth. He felt another wave of misery as he remembered how easily he had given up his remote to this man.

"Since he stole Danny's remote, the Space Twister has been using it to rob banks, steal planes and generally wreak havoc."

Something beeped in Uncle Charlie's pocket. He pulled out a small black phone and glanced at it. "For example, it looks like he's just stolen the *Mona Lisa* and replaced it with a photo of a cat dressed as Elvis."

Uncle Charlie sniggered. "Sorry," he added quickly. "Not funny."

"But how did he take my remote?" cried Danny. "I'd paused time."

"Well, we're not sure," replied Uncle Charlie, "but we think he can twist space."

"Yeah," said Mia, frowning, "I got that from the name, but what does it mean?"

"It means he can twist himself out of time," said Uncle Charlie. "We know he's been trying to do it for years. To stop himself from getting older. To make himself immortal. At first, he was experimenting with giant magnets, trying to pull the earth backwards. Impossible, of course. But then about a year ago, he started endurance training — slowing down his heartbeat and metabolism. Last autumn, at midnight, when the clocks went back, we believe he managed to get halfway out."

"Halfway?" repeated Mia.

"Yes, half his body was out of time. Danny, it's like when you press Pause on your remote. Half of his body had stepped into that place. The trouble was, the other half hadn't. And time was still moving. It nearly pulled him apart. That's why he's got that scar."

Danny and Mia shuddered.

Eric said, "Ouch."

"It runs all the way down the centre of his body," said Uncle Charlie. "From that moment, we think he gave up on space-twisting and tried to find other ways of stopping time. Which is why he stole the remote."

"But he can't have given up on space twisting," said Danny. "He must have done it. He must have got all the way out. Or he couldn't have stolen my remote."

"Maybe," said Uncle Charlie. "The thing

is, we've looked at all our monitors and charts. There's been no major energy distortions this month. Nothing to suggest he pulled himself all the way out of time. But you're right. He must have done. We just don't know how. Or when. Or why we didn't notice."

"Great," growled Mia.

"Basically, we got caught out on this one," said Uncle Charlie. "We should have taken the Space Twister more seriously. We should have warned Danny he might come for the remote. So look, if you want to call me a dingbat or clip me round the ear, do it now."

Danny mumbled, "It's OK."

Mia said, "Dingbat. Nincompoop."

Uncle Charlie waited another couple of seconds then continued to speak. "Right, now that's out of the way, it's time for action. We have to find a way to get Danny's remote back. Or build another one. We're lost while the Space Twister has control over time."

"Is that what was in the parcel?" asked Eric. "Another remote?"

"What parcel?" asked Uncle Charlie.

"The one you just sent us," said Mia.

"These two huge men in dark glasses came along and squashed it," said Eric.

"Oh? Oh!" exclaimed Uncle Charlie. "No, no, that was your birthday present, Mia. A TN50X. You remember Eric's robot, Magnus? It was like that but with artificial intelligence."

"Cool!" said Eric.

"Right," said Mia. "Uncle Charlie, I don't even like robots."

"Don't you?" said Uncle Charlie. "Ah, OK. Well, good job they squashed it, then. But hang on, that's interesting. The two huge men in dark glasses could be the Space Twister's goons. He must have known about the parcel and rewound time to intercept it."

"That's what I said!" exclaimed Danny.

"Which means he thought what was in the parcel was important. I wonder what we did with it?"

"But wasn't it just a toy? How could it have helped us?" asked Danny.

"It seems unlikely, I have to admit," said Uncle Charlie. He looked at Mia, who was scowling. "Maybe Mia threw it at his head. But listen, the main thing to focus on is the fact that we must've had him on the ropes once before. And that means we can do it again – and beat him this time. Only my latest plan doesn't involve any robots."

Uncle Charlie ran over to the window. "Come on, there's no time to lose. We've got to get back to EUREKA! headquarters."

"Er," said Mia, "the door's that way."

"No, no, we'll be using sky ropes," said Uncle Charlie.

"What are they?" asked Danny.

"They're how I got here," said his uncle. "You know how every EUREKA! agent has their own gadget? Well, these are mine. They're the future of public transport."

He pulled two small white arrowheads out of his pocket. They had two large buttons on the side.

Danny and Mia ran across to join their uncle

at the window, but Eric hung back.

"Hang on, hang on," said Eric. "I can't just disappear without telling my mum. Not with all these disasters happening."

"Hmm, yes, good point," said Uncle Charlie, rummaging around in his coat pocket and pulling out a piece of paper. "Leave this for your mum. It's a standard EUREKA! letter. Guaranteed to set her mind at rest."

Eric took the piece of paper and glanced at its contents. It read:

Dear parent or carer

Your son/daughter is accompanying a EUREKA! agent on a top secret mission. We take full responsibility for any gruesome injury they may suffer.

Eric shrugged and said, "Fair enough."

Uncle Charlie stepped on to the windowsill and pressed a button on the side of one of the white arrowheads. A thick beam of light shot out of the end.

"Right, this is how we'll do this," he said. "Eric, you hold on to my left arm. Danny, you hold on to my right arm. Mia, you hang on to my back."

"We what?" said Mia.

"It's perfectly safe," added Uncle Charlie.

The three children looked at each other and then scrambled out of the window. Eric glanced up at the thick white tube that Uncle Charlie was hanging on to. It stretched up into the sky and out of sight.

"Hang on," said Uncle Charlie.

He pressed a button on the side of the white cable and the four of them were pulled up into the sky at immense speed.

Within **two seconds**, they could see the whole of their town; within **four seconds**, they could see the fields and forests that surrounded it. After about ten seconds, Uncle Charlie slid the button upwards and they stopped moving.

"Sky ropes are a bit like tape measures," he said. "They can be wound up or wound out. I just wound this one up. That's why we shot upwards."

He squinted at another cloud.

"The other thing to say is travelling by sky rope is also a bit like swinging through the jungle on vines. And just like swinging through the jungle, you need two vines to get anywhere."

He pulled out the second white arrowhead.

"I'm going to aim this second sky rope at that cloud over there. When the arrowhead hits, it should react with the water vapour and become a solid block of matter, enough to support up to nine people. Then we'll hang on to that one and retract this one. Takes a while to get used to, so hold tight."

Danny, Mia and Eric hadn't heard a word

of what Uncle Charlie had just said. Mia was staring at her feet, Danny was staring at the ground below, Eric was looking up at the cloud they were hanging from.

Uncle Charlie pressed the button on the other sky rope and a white cable shot across the sky and latched on to the next cloud along. At the same time, he held down the button on the first sky rope so that it shrank back to nothing – just an arrowhead.

They swung through the sky, getting faster and faster. As the cable swung out to its furthest point, Charlie aimed at the next cloud and fired out another length of sky rope. They swung on this cloud, then Charlie aimed again, and they swung from the next one. For a while, the clouds got further apart, and they swung lower and longer and slower. Then the clouds got thicker, and the wind picked up, and they swung in loops and zigzags, riding the sudden gusts.

"The clouds over there are moving fast, and moving east," said Uncle Charlie. "We can ride one of them the rest of the way."

He swung them towards a thick band of swiftly moving cloud. He latched on to the thickest, fastest, lowest cloud and just swung back and forth on it. The sky rope acted like a pendulum, moving slower and slower until it finally stopped. Now it was just the movement of the cloud that pulled them through the sky, towing them slowly eastwards.

Danny, Mia and Eric had got more used to travelling by sky rope now. They were looking into the distance and grinning.

"What do you do when there aren't any clouds?" asked Eric.

"Get the bus," said Uncle Charlie with a shrug.

A flock of birds appeared just below their feet, keeping pace with them as they moved further east.

"Hang on, I've got to time this right," said Uncle Charlie.

He slid the sky rope button down and the cable started to get longer, sending them towards the earth at a swift pace.

"Uncle Charlie, this feels dangerous!" shouted Danny, as the wind roared in his ears.

"That's because it is dangerous," Uncle Charlie shouted back.

Danny, Mia and Eric looked down at the large field that was rushing up to meet them.

When they were about ten metres from the grass, Uncle Charlie slid the button down one notch further and they stopped dropping so quickly.

"OK, let go," said Uncle Charlie.

They all landed gently in the field, taking a few steps to steady themselves. Then they burst into relieved laughter.

Uncle Charlie put the two white arrowheads back in his pocket.

"OK, guys, could you stand in the middle of that patch of daisies?" asked Uncle Charlie.

Danny, Mia and Eric nodded, still laughing slightly.

"Kombooshya Kombooshya Jimi Hendrix Tumble Dryer," said Uncle Charlie. Then he clapped his hands together. There was a whirring sound underneath them. The disc of grass they were standing on started to move downwards.

"Just stand perfectly still," said Uncle Charlie. They watched as roots and earth and rocks and clay moved past them.

Eric looked back up the narrow shaft. "What if a sheep wanders past and falls in?" he asked.

"As long as it's not an evil robot sheep," replied Uncle Charlie, "then we don't mind."

The lift continued to move down through the earth. They passed a thick slab of granite and then a cave opened out in front of them and the disc of grass came slowly to rest on the ground.

Danny, Mia and Eric gazed at the scene in front of them.

"Let's step off before we're crushed by falling sheep," said Uncle Charlie.

They moved forward and the grassy lift rose back up behind them, climbing slowly towards the surface.

They found themselves in a huge cave,

perhaps a hundred metres deep and fifty metres high. The ground was damp under their feet and there was a musty smell in the air. But in every other way, this was like no cave they had ever seen. Wherever they looked, they saw ridges and clusters of beautiful crystals. On the roof, the crystals seemed to be a bright red; on the far wall, they looked a dark green. The crystals beside them gave off a luminous white glow. But elsewhere the crystals were all jumbled up: purple beside yellow next to black on top of pink. In the middle of the cave, a small lake reflected all of the light and colour back at the crystals and out into the air, making the whole chamber as bright and clear as a village square at noon.

"This is EUREKA!'s new headquarters?" asked Mia, still staring at the crystals above her head.

"Since about an hour ago, yes," said Uncle Charlie. "You know how Danny's cosmic remote has an amber crystal in its back? That's what gives it its power?"

Mia nodded.

"Well, the man who invented the cosmic remote originally found the amber crystal in this cave. So we thought we might as well set up camp here while we look for another one. As I said, if we can make another cosmic remote, we may be able to beat the Space Twister."

"We'll beat him all right," said a voice from the back of the cave.

"He'll have more than one scar when we've finished with him," said another voice.

"Jasper! Roxie!" exclaimed Danny.

A young man with sticky-up hair and huge headphones round his neck and a young woman wearing a blue wig and a luminous green skirt appeared next to Uncle Charlie. Roxie gave Danny, Eric and Mia a big hug each. Jasper just saluted and said, "Hey."

"You found any crystals yet?" Uncle Charlie asked them.

"Oh, yeah. About that," said Roxie. "What colour was the crystal in the back of the remote again?"

"Amber," said Uncle Charlie.

"Amber," said Jasper. "That's sort of green, isn't it?"

"Orange," said Uncle Charlie.

"I told you it was orange," said Jasper.

"I told YOU it was orange," said Roxie.

"So," said Uncle Charlie, "which of you two 'elite EUREKA! agents' wants to start the briefing?"

Roxie and Jasper glanced at each other. "You do the Time Tablet," said Roxie. "I'll do the other two."

Jasper nodded. "Makes sense."

Roxie said, "Let me borrow your TS Player." She took the headphones from around Jasper's neck.

"Hey!" said Jasper. "Hold them by the speakers, not the wires."

Roxie put them on and her head started to bob. "Tell me when it's my bit, Jaspo."

Jasper sighed, and turned to Danny, Eric and Mia. "Time to hand out some gadgets."

3
RESTART

"So Charlie told you about the Space Twister, right?" said Jasper. Danny and Mia nodded.

"Ahem," said Eric. "You mentioned gadgets?"

"I did," said Jasper. He had a rucksack over one of his shoulders. He swung it down on to the floor.

"So, you need to be able to defend yourselves against the Space Twister," said Jasper. "He knows that EUREKA! will try to get the remote back. He'll do anything he can to find our headquarters and he'll do whatever it takes to neutralise any EUREKA! agents."

"What's neutralise?" asked Eric. "Isn't it what happens to dogs to stop them having puppies? I could really do without that."

"It means do you in, bump you off, take you out," said Mia, rolling her eyes.

"But we're not EUREKA! agents," said Danny.

"If he finds you with us, he'll assume you are," said Uncle Charlie.

"So why bring us here?" asked Eric.

"Because you're still safer here than you would be out there," said Uncle Charlie.

"But nowhere is entirely safe," said Jasper. "The Space Twister's powers are immense. If he finds you, you need to be able to escape fast, before he's had a chance to pause or rewind or fast forward."

Jasper put his hand in the rucksack and pulled out a thin slab of glass with rounded edges.

"One Time Tablet," he said, handing it to Danny.

Jasper pulled out a large silver key with an ornate handle.

"One Mirror Key," he said, giving it to Mia.

Jasper removed a plastic bottle of red spray with a speech bubble printed on the side.

"One can of Truth Spray," he said, tossing it to Eric.

Danny, Eric and Mia looked at their gadgets for a few seconds.

"Jasper," said Mia finally, "it looks like you've given us a pane of glass, a key with nothing to open and a bottle of deodorant."

Eric was sniffing one of his armpits. "I had a bath the week before last," he muttered to himself.

"Prepare to have your minds blown," said Jasper. "Prepare to have your heads stretched and your brains melted. Let's start with Danny.

Put your thumb in the small dent in the bottom right-hand side of the glass."

Danny did this and a screen appeared inside the small curved pane of glass. It showed a map of the world with a magnifying glass in the top right and a search box in the top left.

Jasper said, "The Time Tablet contains a description of every human being currently living on Planet Earth. Everyone's story is in there, from presidents to street sweepers. You can find people geographically by using the map. Or if you know people's names, you can search for them by typing their name in that box in the top left."

"This can't be possible," said Danny.

"Search for me, search for me," said Eric.

Danny scanned the map and touched the UK. The map expanded and an outline of the UK filled the screen. Danny touched the South East, and then Surrey, and then his home town. At this point, a list of small folders appeared, showing all the streets in his home town: Abacus Street, Ardsley Road, Ash Tree Terrace and so on. Danny clicked on his street, and another list of folders appeared; this time, they had people's faces on them and their names underneath. There were his parents, **HECTOR DANGER** and **MURIEL DANGER**.

"Where are me and Mia?" asked Danny.

"Well, you're not there, are you?" said Jasper. "Your folders will be in your current location. Which is Hawksby Caves in Humberside."

Danny nodded and used the map to find Hawksby Caves. There were six folders inside: **CHARLES BAKER, ROXANNE CLARKE, JASPER GIBBONS, ERIC TAYLOR, MIA DANGER** and **DANIEL DANGER.**

Danny clicked on his own name.

The screen was filled with words. The first sentence read:

Daniel Danger was born at 05:19 on the 9th September 2002. He was born in St Hubert's Hospital under the care of Dr Vikram Malik and Nurse Margery Patterson.

"Scroll further down," said Jasper.

Danny dragged his finger down the screen.

Words whizzed past. Danny lifted his finger off the screen. He had stopped at a passage that read:

The bald man stepped off the bottom stair and swivelled on his heel.

"Now, let me guess," he drawled. "Charles Baker's son — or nephew — or younger brother?"

Danny didn't reply.

"Oh well, it's of no importance," sniffed the Night Scientist. "Just hand me the cosmic remote and I'll leave you and your family in peace."

Danny scrolled further down.

The parrots had swept Danny, Eric and Mia into the sky. Each of the children had one parrot clinging to their left shoulder and one parrot clinging to their right shoulder.

"This is my life," murmured Danny.

Jasper nodded and smiled. "Have a look at the end."

Danny stroked the screen faster. The crystals on the cave wall twinkled on the screen. Danny got to the last sentence.

The crystals on the cave wall twinkled on the screen. Danny got to the last sentence.

As Danny was reading, another sentence appeared one letter at a time.

As Danny was reading, another sentence appeared one letter at a time.

"It updates every second," said Jasper. "Pretty clever stuff, eh? There's an entry like that for every person on the planet."

"How is this even possible?" said Danny.

"It tunes into people's brainwaves," said Jasper. "Picks up all the electrical impulses and converts them into narrative using a basic CDN codec and a bespoke nano-transponder. Brilliantly simple."

Eric had been watching over Danny's shoulder. "So let's just put the Space Twister's name in there," he said. "Find out where he is and get Danny's remote back."

Jasper looked up at Uncle Charlie.

"We don't know his real name," said Uncle Charlie. "And we don't know where he is. So

I'm afraid we can't use the Time Tablet to find him."

"Or we'd have done it already, right?" Jasper added.

"Hey, look up Mr Boswell," said Eric. "We can find out where he's put my inflatable Martian. You remember, he confiscated it before Christmas."

"Yeah," said Danny, "then we can look up Stephen Tweep. I'm sure he stole my MangaBoy T-shirt when we were doing PE."

Mia looked at the Time Tablet and then down at the key in her hand. "So Danny gets a computer that reads people's minds and I get … this."

Uncle Charlie chuckled. "If you thought sky ropes were fun, just wait till you start using mirrors to get about."

Jasper gave Roxie a nudge. Her eyes were closed and she was nodding her head energetically.

"Oi, crackpot, you're on," he said, giving her another nudge.

Roxie took the headphones off and said,

"Wow, these cans are awesome, Jasp. It's like getting new ears."

"Give," said Jasper, slinging them round his neck. "You have to tell Mia about her key now."

"Sure thing," said Roxie. "A Mirror Key is about as good as gadgets get. It lets you use any mirror in the world as a portal. You can then travel to any other mirror you like."

Danny and Eric had stopped looking at the Time Tablet and were listening to Roxie. Mia was starting to smile.

"I've propped up a mirror against the far wall," said Roxie, "and there's a smaller one over there behind that boulder. You're going to travel from one to the other." Roxie grabbed Mia's hand. "It's OK, I'll go with you the first time."

Roxie and Mia trotted across to the furthest mirror with Danny and the others following close behind.

Roxie rapped on the glass. "It's an ordinary mirror. Move your key across the surface."

Mia held the key about a centimetre away

from the mirror's surface and moved it round in circles.

"There," said Roxie.

"Where?" said Mia.

"There," said Roxie. "Back a bit."

Mia moved the key up slightly and a faint keyhole shape appeared on the mirror. She kept the key steady and the outline grew darker and harder until an actual keyhole took shape.

"It's never more than a few centimetres away from the centre," said Roxie. "You'll soon be finding it with your eyes closed."

Mia glanced at Roxie and then put the key in the keyhole, turning it one way and then the other. There was a click.

"Shall we go in?" said Roxie.

The surface of the mirror seemed to quiver.

"What's in there?" asked Mia.

"Only one way to find out," said Roxie.

Roxie put her leg into the mirror. A small silver wave rippled out towards the frame. Danny, Eric and Mia watched, their mouths half open. Roxie put her other leg forward and vanished. A split second later, her arm came out of the mirror and beckoned.

Uncle Charlie smiled and said, "Go for it, Mia. Take the boys with you if you like."

Mia frowned and nodded.

"I'm coming with you, Mia," said Danny.

"I'll, er, stay here and look after the cave," said Eric.

Mia put one foot into the mirror. "This feels deeply weird," she said.

She seemed to take a deep breath and then stepped through the glass. A large ripple passed over the surface of the mirror and died away.

"OK, let's go," said Danny. He put down the Time Tablet and grabbed Eric's arm.

"No, seriously, Danny," Eric protested. "I'll talk to your uncle about chaos theory or something."

Danny gave Eric a gentle shove into the mirror. Then he picked up his Time Tablet and jumped through after him.

He felt as if he'd been dipped in a lake of ice. Then the sensation passed and he found himself in a small grey room with no doors or windows.

Behind him, he saw the full-length mirror that had been hanging on the wall of the cave. Mia, Eric and Roxie were standing next to him.

"Where are we?" asked Eric.

"The control room," replied Roxie. "Like what they've done with it? Now, Mia, to activate the lightning drive, you've got to lock the mirror."

"Lock it?" asked Mia.

"Yeah, that mirror's still open until you do," said Roxie. "Anyone can get through."

"OK," said Mia, and she held the key up to the mirror. She located the keyhole again, slotted the key in, and turned it the other way. There was a thunk as the lock slid into place.

"Well done," said Roxie. "Now, to sign in as the Mirror Key's owner, you say this: '*Mirror, mirror, on the wall, Come to life whenever I call*'."

Mia repeated the rhyme.

A middle-aged woman's face appeared in the centre of the mirror. She had round glasses, curly grey hair and large hoops in her ears.

"Hello, darlings," she said. "Where are we

off to?"

"You give your instructions to this woman," said Roxie. "She's a computer simulation. Understands most ordinary words and phrases."

"And look, you can change her settings!" exclaimed Eric, pointing to a set of touchscreen buttons and sliders that had appeared at the bottom of the mirror.

"Cool!" said Danny and Mia.

"Friendliness is on its maximum setting," said Eric. "Let's make her UNfriendly."

"You can change her into a man, too," said Mia, "and make her really old or really young."

Roxie sighed and said, "This mirror can beam you across the world, you know."

Danny, Mia and Eric weren't listening.

"Make her talk in Norwegian!" said Eric.

"Make her skin-colour blue!" added Danny.

They settled on a young man with green skin, one Cyclops eye and dreadlocks. They gave him the name Umberto. His personality was set to Moderately Friendly.

"Finished?" asked Roxie. "Now tell it where

you want to go."

"Er, OK," said Mia. "The other side of the cave, please."

"Piece of cake," said Umberto, closing his eye.

The mirror gave off a burst of white light, like a camera flash. Then the frame started to move inwards, whirring and crunching, shrinking the mirror's surface. The mirror ended up about a metre wide and a metre tall. It was hanging halfway up the wall.

"That's the other mirror," said Roxie. "Mia, want to do the honours?"

Mia smiled and unlocked the mirror.

"How does all of this work?" asked Eric. "Did we teleport? Did we move at all?"

"Sorry, Eric," said Roxie, "you'll have to ask Jasper. He understands all that boring stuff. I've just come along for the ride."

She ducked down and put her head through the mirror. Quick as a flash, she pulled it back out again. She whipped a catapult out of her pocket, loaded a pellet into it and stretched the rubber band back. Danny remembered that catapult from the last time he had met Roxie. It had blasted robot animals to pieces.

"No one say a word," whispered Roxie.

She continued to aim the catapult at the mirror. Mia, Eric and Danny stood silently in the grey room, listening to each other's breathing.

"OK, look," said Roxie. "There were two heavies in the cave. Shaved heads, dark glasses, cheap suits. I think one of them saw me."

"That sounds like the men who came to our house!" whispered Danny.

"OK, that confirms it," said Roxie. "The Space Twister sent them. Thing is, there's no sign of Charlie or Jasper. So listen. I'm going in there to take them out. You stay here. Lock this mirror. If I don't knock on it in ten minutes, leave. Get as far away as you can. Somewhere the Space Twister will never find you."

"Wait!" Danny exclaimed.

But Roxie had already leapt through the mirror, shouting, "Let's rock 'n' roll!"

Danny spun round. "We've got to help her,"

he said.

"She said wait," replied Mia.

"But what about Uncle Charlie?"

"She said **WAIT**," repeated Mia.

"She said lock the mirror, too," said Eric. "Remember they can still get through."

"Leave it open," said Danny. "I'm going in. You two can do what you want."

"No, Danny, no," said Mia. "You're ten years old! They'll snap you like a twig."

"I don't care," said Danny, running forward. Mia held him more tightly and Eric grabbed his other arm.

They struggled for a few seconds.

"OK, Danny, listen," said Mia. "We'll quickly put our heads through. See what's going on."

"Bad idea," said Eric. "They'll pull us through by our hair."

"It'll be, like, two seconds," said Mia. "A quick look, then back in again, OK?"

Danny grunted.

"Eric?" said Mia.

Eric sighed.

They lined up next to each other and put their heads through the mirror.

The cave was empty, just crystals twinkling and the pool of water glinting.

"Oh no," murmured Danny and he leapt into the cave.

"Danny!" whispered Mia, following him in.

"Stop!" exclaimed Eric, staying where he was, his head poking out of the mirror.

Danny and Mia were standing by the edge of the pool, their eyes fixed on an object floating in the middle of the water. It was Roxie's catapult.

"They've got her," said Danny.

"Maybe – maybe she escaped," said Mia. "We don't know what happened."

"I told you we should have helped her," said Danny.

"What are you two talking about?" shouted

Eric, his head still sticking out of the mirror.

"You can come out now, Eric," said Mia. "There's no one here."

Eric glanced around the cave. "I'll think about it," he said.

"Th-they've got Roxie and Jasper and Uncle Charlie," stammered Danny. "Where have they taken them? And how do we get there?"

Danny looked down at the sheet of glass in his hand and the large shiny key in Mia's.

He switched on the Time Tablet and tapped it frantically.

"I'll look up Uncle Charlie," said Danny. "Roxie and Jasper will probably be with him. And then we can use your key to go and get them."

Mia was about to raise an objection, but realised she didn't have any. "Good idea," she said.

Danny found Charles Theobald Baker and clicked on his folder. As Danny was scrolling to the end of the document, Eric appeared quietly between them. They all read the words together.

Roxie led the three children into the mirror, leaving Charlie and Jasper alone in the cave.

"While they're in there," said Charlie, "let's keep looking for amber crystals."

"Seriously?" said Jasper.

Charlie nodded.

Jasper sighed and put on his headphones. He began to search through mounds of crystals using direct matter transfer — picking them up and setting them down using nothing but brainpower.

"I forgot he could do that," said Eric. "You know, move stuff around with his mind."

"Shh," said Mia. "I'm trying to read."

Jasper was listening to very loud music. This meant that he didn't notice the two thugs till they were holding him down and searching his pockets.

Jasper picked them both up using direct matter transfer and held them upside-down over the lake.

"Jasper!" said Charlie. "We have to leave. Now."

"Why?" asked Jasper. "I'm in complete control of the situation."

"Don't you get it?" said Charlie. "The Space Twister

sent them. All they have to do is tell him where we are and he'll pause time and come and get us."

"Let me throw them in the lake then," said Jasper.

"They're bound to have a system in place," said Charlie, "like when we send agents out. If the Space Twister doesn't hear from them every ten or twenty minutes, he'll assume something's wrong. Again, he'll pause time. Jasper, we have to run. We can't fight him yet. We have to hide."

"What about the kids?" asked Jasper.

"Roxie's with them," said Charlie, "and Danny will read this on his Time Tablet."

"You sure?" asked Jasper.

"Positive," said Uncle Charlie. "Danny, I know you're reading this. Find Grace Bingley. She lives in York. Use the Mirror Key to get there. We think that the Space Twister visited her three months ago, but we've no idea why. Try to find out. This is our Plan B. There is no Plan C."

"You sure I can't drop them in the lake?" asked Jasper.

"No," said Charlie. "Put them down. Drop their phones in the lake. And follow me."

Charlie ran over to the lift. He heard a groan and a

splash and then Jasper appeared next to him.

As the lift started to rise, he saw Roxie putting her head out of the second mirror.

"Where are we going?" asked Jasper.

"There are five other places with reported sightings of crystals," said Uncle Charlie. "We've got to check out all of them."

The lift reached the surface and Charlie whipped his sky ropes out of his pocket. Jasper put his arms round Charlie's shoulders.

"You on?" asked Charlie.

"I'm on," said Jasper.

Charlie fired a rope into the nearest cloud and the two of them shot into the sky.

Danny, Eric and Mia stopped reading and looked at each other. Another sentence appeared at the end of Uncle Charlie's story.

Within five minutes, Charlie and Jasper were flying over Manchester.

"He's OK," said Danny.

"But what about Roxie?" asked Mia.

"We could look her up," said Danny. "What's

her surname? Her folder was on the screen with her name underneath."

But none of them could remember.

"Well, Charlie's told us what to do," said Mia. "Find Grace Bingley. Come on, no time to lose."

Danny and Mia moved towards the mirror, but Eric stayed where he was.

"Come on, Eric," said Danny.

"I thought your uncle might – you know – use the Time Tablet to—"

"What?" asked Danny.

"What?" asked Mia.

"Tell me what my ruddy gadget does!" He held up the bottle he'd been given. "I mean," he said, "you've got a Time Tablet. Mia's got a Mirror Key. What is this?"

"We'll try it out later, Eric," said Danny.

"Yeah, come on bogbreath, we've got to go," said Mia.

Danny and Mia ran towards the mirror, with Eric trudging slowly and sadly behind them.

4
SEARCH

Danny, Mia and Eric were back inside the small grey room.

Mia had locked the mirror and summoned Umberto, the one-eyed man with green skin. "Where are we off to next, kids?" he asked.

"Does Grace Bingley have any mirrors? She lives in York," said Mia.

The man in the mirror stroked his chin. It was clearly an animation that the simulation software ran when it was finding new data.

"Nineteen," he said, "but only five you could actually fit through. Unless you fancy crawling out of the wing mirror of a Ford Focus."

Danny had found Grace Bingley in the Time Tablet.

"I can't work out why the Space Twister would be visiting her," he said, pulling the words down the screen. "I've gone back two weeks now. All she seems to do is eat biscuits and watch game shows."

"She sounds all right," said Eric.

"I've found the ideal mirror," said the green man. "It's at the top of the stairs. A metre and a half tall. Soft carpet on the other side. Enjoy your trip."

"Great," said Mia. The frame whirred and purred as it grew taller, and then clicked loudly into place. Mia placed the key in the mirror and unlocked it.

Mia went through first, then Danny, then Eric. They found themselves on a fairly small landing, in a fairly small house. There was a flight of stairs in front of them and a bathroom behind them. A television was on downstairs.

Mia pointed at the stairs. Danny and Eric nodded.

As they went down, Danny glanced at the pictures and objects on the wall. There was a framed Olympic medal; there was a large photo of a young woman crossing a finishing line with a smile on her face; there was an even bigger photo of the same woman on an Olympic podium. She was standing on Number One, wearing gold.

As they crossed the hall, they could hear the television more clearly. A newsreader was saying: **"...the latest in a string of mysterious disasters: the MARMITE factory in Manchester has been burnt to the ground. While down in Slough, the factory that makes two thirds of the UK's FISH PASTE was also in flames..."**

They heard someone tutting in the room where the television was.

"She's in the living room," whispered Mia.

They all tiptoed gently towards the living-room door and pushed it open. They saw an old lady sitting in a large red armchair, opposite an old-fashioned television.

Without turning round, the old lady said, "I knew you'd come."

Danny and Mia looked at each other.

"I've been expecting you for some time," the old lady added.

Danny took a step towards her.

The old lady turned round and a look of surprise crossed her face. "Oh, my word! Who are you? I thought you were meals on wheels."

"Oh, ah, no," stammered Danny.

"Well, what's going on, then? I've been looking forward to my devilled kidneys all morning."

"Er, I don't know," said Danny. "I think everything's a bit upside down."

The old lady gestured at the television. "Load of nonsense," she said. "They should try having both kneecaps replaced. Then they'd actually have something to complain about."

It was then that Danny realised how old the woman actually was. She had a mug on the table next to her with 100 YEARS YOUNG painted on it. Next to the mug, there were a pair of glasses with incredibly thick lenses and a tube of false teeth adhesive.

"Erm, I'm sorry, ah, Mrs Bingley," said Mia,

"but we're in a bit of a rush. We think that someone called the Space Twister visited you. Do you remember him?"

"Does he do meals on wheels?"

"I don't think so," said Mia.

"Then he can jump off a bridge for all I care," said Mrs Bingley.

Mia tried again. "He would have had black hair. And a scar down the middle of his face."

"Oh, him!" exclaimed Mrs Bingley. "He was a very, very rude man. And yes, a face to wake the dead. I soon sent him about his business."

"So he didn't ask you anything?" pressed Danny. "You didn't tell him anything?"

"No I didn't," said Mrs Bingley. "Years ago, I'd have the press camping outside my house, so I'm quite good at telling people to clear off. And now I'm telling you!"

"You had people camping outside?" asked Eric.

Danny suddenly remembered the photos on the stairs. He looked into Mrs Bingley's eyes.

"Is that you in all those photos, Mrs Bingley? The ones in the hall?"

Mrs Bingley sighed. "Yep. Didn't need people to bring me food in them days. Could fetch my own tea. Wouldn't take me two minutes to jog to the caff."

"You mean, you ran in races and stuff?" asked Eric.

"One or two," said Mrs Bingley. "A couple of those Olympics thingies. A Commonwealth whatsit. Half a dozen of those marathon doodahs. Ooh yes. I did like to feel the wind in my hair, the air on my cheeks."

"Must have been brilliant," said Eric.

"It wasn't half bad," said Mrs Bingley. "And guess what they used to call me?"

"Er, er," pondered Eric. "Racy Gracey?"

"The Bullet," said Mrs Bingley. "Can you imagine? Me! A Bullet! Tell you what, I've got a bit of video of me back in the day. Young lady, can you see that tape on the side there. Well, what you've got to do is pop it in that machine. It's called a video recorder. It's very clever."

They had an old-fashioned video recorder at Mia's school so she knew how it worked. A picture soon flickered up on the screen. Everyone had wonky teeth and incredibly neat hair. Six women were crouching down on the starting line of a race track. Cheerful music was playing and a posh voice was talking over it: **"Now hyah we are at the start of the women's hundred metres. And in lane number three, Britain's very own Grace Bingley. Let's see if she can *smesh* another record."**

The pistol was fired and something extraordinary happened. Grace Bingley – the woman in lane number three – became a blur. She literally shot through the air. She became visible again just before she crossed the finishing line. The other five women in the race weren't even halfway along the track.

"H-how did you do that?" stammered Eric.

"I don't know," said Mrs Bingley. "I just

went as fast as I could. Concentrated really hard. It was strange, it was almost like time slowed down when I was running."

"OK," said Danny quietly. "Now I get it."

"I'm beginning to get it, too," said Mia.

"Oh, er, yeah," added Eric. "I get it, too. Definitely. I mean, I really get it. I seriously get it."

"Mrs Bingley," said Danny, "this is really important. When you say you slowed down time, what were you actually doing?"

"Well, er, it was a long time ago, young man," said Mrs Bingley, "but I suppose I just focused on the finishing line. And how much I wanted to reach it first. And then when the pistol went, I latched on to that noise – the echo of the pistol – and imagined myself stretching it so everything would take longer, everything would get slower. And in my head, everything was slower. When I glanced at the other racers, they were sort of in slow motion."

She bit her bottom lip and closed her eyes. She opened them again and said, "It's like, say I want to close the back door. I can see that filthy cat from next door trying to creep in and do his business on the lino. So I sort of – concentrate on the door and the noise from the TV and try and – look it's difficult – you see I'd – ee, I'm not as young as I was – what I'd do is –"

Mrs Bingley became a blur, leaving a trail of white and blue hanging in the air. The back door clicked shut and another ribbon of bright colour rippled across the room. Grace Bingley was back in the armchair, taking deep breaths.

"I didn't go too fast that time," said Mrs Bingley. "Walking pace really. I'm a hundred and four years old, my dears."

"That is the most amazing thing I've ever seen a really old person do," said Eric. "By some distance."

"OK, so we know why the Space Twister came here three months ago," said Mia. "He wanted Mrs Bingley to show him how to do that."

Danny nodded. "You can control time, Mrs Bingley."

"Control who?" said Mrs Bingley. "I don't think so, dear. Not me, dear. Sorry, dear. Got me mixed up with someone else, dear."

"You can," said Danny. "You're a sort of Space Twister."

"No, dear," said Mrs Bingley. "I'm just really blooming fast. Or at least I was. You young people have a funny name for everything these days. Space Twister indeed."

Danny was staring at the floor, lost in his own thoughts. Finally he said, "I've done it."

"What's that, mate?" said Eric.

"I've done it," said Danny again. "I've done what Mrs Bingley just did."

"What do you mean, Danny?" asked Mia.

"When I was duelling with the Night Scientist," said Danny. "You remember, when we both had cosmic remotes. I remember being able to feel time. See, he'd press Rewind and I'd have to press Fast Forward at that second to cancel it. And I could feel time starting to go backwards – I could feel it grab hold of me – and I had to break free of it so I could press Fast

Forward. I only did it for a second but I did it."

"Blimey," said Eric.

Danny looked up at Mia and Eric. "That's how we beat him. I have to learn how to twist space."

"Hold on, Danny," said Mia.

"It's the only way," said Danny. "Otherwise I'll never get my remote back. Mrs Bingley, will you teach me?"

"No way, Danny, absolutely no way," said Mia. "We're not talking about learning how to play the saxophone here. This is dangerous. The Space Twister was nearly torn in half."

"But I did it," insisted Danny. "And I'm fine."

"Put a sock in it, the lot of you," said Mrs Bingley, making them jump. "Now, allow me to clear up a couple of things. First of all, no, I won't teach you how to do it. Even if I wanted to, I couldn't. You either know it or you don't."

The video of the Olympics had stopped and the news had come back on again. A news reporter was standing in front of Bond Street tube station in London. The headline read:

LONDON ANTIQUES DEALER VANISHES ALONG WITH EVERYTHING IN HIS SHOP

"Secondly," said Mrs Bingley, "I'm about to throw you out. You've all got lovely faces, especially you, dear." She pointed at Eric, who blushed. "But I don't know who you are and, as I said to that rude man with the ugly mug ... oooh! There he is on me telly!"

Danny, Mia and Eric turned round and saw the Space Twister standing outside a London store, being interviewed by a smiley young woman with a severe bob.

"I had just bought this adorable Victorian sugar bowl," said the Space Twister. "It breaks my heart to think I'll never get the matching tongs."

"So you didn't see anything?" asked the smiley interviewer.

"No, whoever did this clearly has special powers of some kind. I'd advise everyone to stay indoors. Keep your children in their rooms." He turned to look directly into the camera. "Leave this one to the grown-ups."

Danny and Mia looked at each other.

"He must mean us," said Eric and shuddered.

Danny was staring at the Space Twister's face. It might have been the camera, but he didn't look like the same man that had taken the remote only a few hours before. He still had the scar, the pale skin, the jewels in his teeth. But his hair had grey streaks in it now, and there were lines around his strangely coloured eyes.

"Thank you for your time, sir," said the interviewer.

"Oh, I have all the time in the world," replied the Space Twister, looking straight at the camera again.

"Hang on," said Danny. "Look, it says it's live TV."

"It does as well," said Mia. "That means he's actually there."

"And he's in front of an antiques shop," said Danny. "There must be dozens of mirrors in there."

"He looks different," said Mrs Bingley, squinting at the TV. "He didn't have those jewels in his mouth. Or such a smart suit."

"Come on," said Danny. "Before he leaves."

"Hang on a minute, Danny," said Mia.

But Danny was already running up the stairs.

"Goodbye, Mrs Bingley," said Mia, and then turned and followed Danny.

"Thanks and all that," said Eric, before running up the stairs too.

Mrs Bingley was left staring at the TV screen. "Davidson," she muttered. "Eric Davidson. That was his name. And what a face he had on him." She whizzed quietly across to the TV and switched it off.

5
MOVE

Danny, Mia and Eric were in the grey room. Umberto was staring blankly at them.

"Now, one second, Danny," said Mia. "Let's think this through."

"We haven't got time!" said Danny. "We've got to go NOW."

"And then what?" said Mia. "We've got no swords or spears or pointy sticks. He's got the remote."

"She's usually wrong," said Eric, "but this time she's right."

Danny looked at the floor. "Maybe I should have stayed with Mrs Bingley. And worked out how to twist space first..." he muttered.

Mia said, "I wouldn't have let you, Danny.

Besides, Mrs Bingley said you can't learn it."

Danny sighed. Then a smile spread across his face. "So we don't try to catch the Space Twister," he said. "We just follow him."

"Eh?" said Eric. "On what? Our invisible motorbikes?"

"No," said Danny. "We use mirrors. We hop from one to another. Hopefully he'll lead us to his hideout. If we know where that is, we can wait till he's asleep and take the remote back."

"Hmm, that might work," said Mia.

"Unless he sees us," said Eric, "or presses Pause. Or goes somewhere with no mirrors. Then it really won't work."

"Please, Mia," said Danny. "We've got to try."

"Ok," she said, turning to Umberto. "Take us to London. It was an antiques shop. The sign said MARMADUKE FARQUAR."

Umberto rolled his single eye. "There are about fifty mirrors in there, including one that takes up half the ceiling."

"That one will do," said Mia.

"OK," said Umberto. "Step right in."

Mia leapt in first, followed by Danny and Eric. When they jumped in, they were upright; as they passed through the mirror, they felt themselves twisted round until they faced the floor. They flew out of the mirror on the ceiling of the shop, and landed on a soft brown carpet. After they'd stood up and brushed themselves off, they realised that they were being stared at by a short, stocky man with gigantic eyebrows.

"How the blazes did you get in here?" he barked.

"Just on our way out," said Danny, hastily.

They looked up and down the busy street and spotted the interviewer with the smiley face. Danny ran up to her.

"Er, hello," he said. "That man you just interviewed. Which way did he go?"

"Why?" she asked.

"Er, he's my dad," said Danny. "I'm an orphan."

"Oh, OK," said the interviewer. "He went

up that street."

As they walked away, Mia said, "You're such a numpty. How can you be an orphan and have a dad?"

"It worked, didn't it?" said Danny.

"That's him!" said Eric in a loud whisper.

The Space Twister was walking up a side street, followed by the two large men they'd seen in the cave.

"He's going into that shop full of statues," said Eric.

"One of his bodyguards is turning round," said Danny.

"Quick!" said Mia, pointing at a mirror leaning against a delivery van. She unlocked it quickly and the three of them stepped through.

"Did you see the name of the shop?" asked Danny.

"Cunningham and Spong," said Eric.

"Ok, are there any mirrors in Cunningham and Spong?" Mia asked Umberto.

"Only two," he replied. "One in the stock room and one behind the till."

"The till it is," said Mia, "but, listen Danny, we're going to be careful. We just peek out."

"OK, OK," said Danny.

Mia put the top of her head gently through the mirror. "Curses, he's already on his way out."

"Let me see," said Danny, pushing Mia out of the way and putting his head through.

"He's crossed the road," said Danny. "There's a mirror in the window of the shop opposite. Let's head for that."

"OK," said Mia. Danny gave Umberto the name of the shop and the three of them put their heads slowly through the mirror again.

They watched the Space Twister and his bodyguards walk past two more buildings and then turn right into a large shopping street.

A couple of passersby had stopped to look at the mirror with Danny, Eric and Mia's heads sticking out of it.

"Very modern," said one passerby. "I'm quite taken with it."

"It's creepy, that's what it is," said another.

"I wouldn't want that hanging over the bed."

Danny, Eric and Mia kept using mirrors in shops, banks and restaurants to follow the Space Twister as he walked through London.

After twenty minutes, Eric put his head out and pulled it sharply back in again. "Lock it, lock it," he whispered. "I'm sure a bodyguard saw me."

"Oh no!" exclaimed Danny. "If the Space Twister suspects anything, he'll go. He'll press Pause and go."

"If he finds out we're using mirrors to get around, that would be bad too," said Mia.

"We'd better check," said Danny. "Maybe the bodyguard didn't see anything, Eric. Maybe he just happened to be looking in this direction."

"Look, just lock the mirror, OK?" said Eric. "I wouldn't stick your head out there unless you want it pulled off."

"All right, all right," said Danny. He thought for a moment. "Maybe we don't have to put our heads through it."

"What do you mean?" asked Eric.

Danny reached into his trouser pocket and fished out a piece of paper. It was the last letter that Uncle Charlie had sent him, a few days before. He rolled it into a tube and held it up to his eye. "Not the greatest periscope in the world, perhaps," he said.

Mia smiled. "Nice," she said.

Eric said, "OK, but put it through one of the bottom corners, not the middle. He'll be looking into the middle."

Danny crouched down by the edge of the mirror and pushed the paper tube through. He put his eye up against one end of the tube. He squinted. He wiggled it up and down.

"All I can see is black," said Danny.

"Black is not a good sign," said Eric.

"Give it here," said Mia. She bent down and put her eye up against the tube. She moved the tube around.

"It's his suit," said Mia. "He's got his back to the mirror. He's standing right up against it."

"How do we get him out of the way?" said Danny.

"Like this," said Mia. She held up her index finger and stuck it through the mirror as fast as she could.

"What are you doing!" shouted Eric.

"He'll just think it's indigestion or something," said Mia.

"Indigestion?" replied Eric. "In his back?"

A split second later, the bodyguard's head reared through the mirror and stared confusedly at the three children.

"OK, lock it, lock it!" yelled Danny.

"How can I lock it if he's in it?" Mia shouted.

"Try!" roared Danny.

Mia ducked round the bodyguard and put her key in the mirror. The bodyguard glanced down and snarled.

Eric was backing away from the mirror. Without really thinking, he took out his bottle of Truth Spray.

"What are you waiting for?" shouted Danny.

"We don't know what it does!" Eric cried.

"What else have we got?" yelled Danny. "Hurry up, he's coming through."

At that moment, Mia finished turning the key and the mirror clicked shut. The bodyguard had got his head and chest through. He looked down and wriggled. He was locked into place, unable to get free. At the same time, Eric squirted Truth Spray into the bodyguard's face.

Umberto's voice could be heard echoing in the room. "Unexpected item in mirror. Please unlock mirror and remove item to proceed."

"What's going on here?" bellowed the bodyguard.

"I don't think your spray did anything, Eric," said Danny, "but at least he can't move."

"I knew I'd got the rubbish gadget," said Eric, looking at it miserably.

"Now what do we do?" said Mia sharply. "We can't get out while he's there."

"Well, maybe if you hadn't poked him, he wouldn't BE there," said Eric.

"Well, maybe if he hadn't spotted you, he wouldn't be there either," said Mia.

"Let me go!" shouted the bodyguard. "I'm really very frightened. One of my legs has gone to sleep. I need the toilet quite badly. And if I'm not home by six, my mum gets really worried."

When the bodyguard finished talking, he looked down at his mouth as if it didn't belong to him.

"What happened there?" asked Danny.

"Why did I say all that?" said the bodyguard, frowning angrily.

"Hang on, Eric," said Mia. "Give him another squirt."

Eric held up the spray and aimed it at the bodyguard's face.

"Tell me your name and address," said Mia.

"Raymond Jackson," said the bodyguard. "19b Babylon Drive, Chertsey CE19 2BK."

The bodyguard looked angrily at his mouth.

"OK," said Mia. "So that's why it's called Truth Spray."

Eric looked at the bottle and grinned. "Fan-flipping-tastic!" He looked up at the bodyguard. "I'm going to give him another burst!"

This time, Eric was holding the bottle the wrong way round and squirted it at himself. "Oh no!" he croaked. "I've given myself a faceful!"

"Well, it looks like one squirt only lasts ten seconds or so," said Mia.

"Yes, but what do I do in the meantime?" said Eric. "I know. I won't talk. Just in case I say something embarrassing, like the fact that I fancy Polly McTavish in 5B or that I go to sleep every night cuddling Teddy, Pinky and Woof." Eric looked down at his mouth. "OH NO!"

"I don't know what you three have done to me," shouted the bodyguard, "but when I get out of here, I'm going to tear you limb from limb!"

"Hang on," said Danny. "This could be a really good thing. The bodyguard can't move and we can make him tell the truth. We could find out some useful stuff."

Mia smiled. "You mean, interrogate him?"

"OK, Eric," said Danny, "try spraying him again. Don't aim it at yourself this time."

"Yeah," said Mia. "Polly McTavish wouldn't be impressed."

Eric groaned and then nodded. He squirted

the Truth Spray at the bodyguard.

"Where's the Space Twister's hideout?" asked Danny.

"He's got three," said the bodyguard. "One in Trinidad, one in Cape Town and one in South Wales. He's probably in South Wales right now and I'm not telling you ANYTHING ELSE!"

"Another squirt, Eric," said Mia.

Eric released another cloud of spray.

"What do you mean, he's in South Wales?" asked Danny.

"About a minute ago," said the bodyguard, "when I said I'd seen something suspicious, he said he was going back to the hideout. He's got some gadget that lets him go places quickly. I've never seen it and I don't know how he does it. And STOP ASKING ME THESE QUESTIONS!"

"Give him a double dose, Eric," said Mia, narrowing her eyes.

Eric sprayed the bodyguard twice.

"I need the Space Twister's name and his

address in Wales," said Danny.

"The hideout's in the Brecon Beacons," the bodyguard said. "Not far from Mountain Hare. I don't know his name. I just call him boss."

"Drat," said Danny. "We need his name."

"You mean to find him in the Time Tablet?" asked Mia.

Danny nodded.

"What about Roxie?" said Mia, looking at the bodyguard. "Will we find her in this hideout?"

"You mean, the girl with blue hair?" said the bodyguard. "She's in the basement. East Wing. Room Seventeen. Behind a grey iron door."

"Let's go," said Danny.

"You'll never beat him," said the bodyguard. "He's incredible. He can do anything. He tells me and Big Terry to close our eyes and when we open them again, we're in a different country. Just like that."

"How do we get him out of the way?" asked Danny.

"I don't want to be a bodyguard any more," said the bodyguard. "I'm going to pack it in and become a florist. Flowers have always been my first love, you see. I'd have marigolds and pansies out the front, sunflowers and lilies inside. Compost out the back. Ray's Bouquets, I'd call it."

"Let's just push him out the way," said Eric. "He's in his own world."

"Oh, but I'm a monster," the bodyguard was whimpering. "Nobody wants to buy gladioli from a monster…"

Mia unlocked the mirror, and Danny and Eric gave the bodyguard a shove. The bodyguard vanished, Mia locked the mirror and Umberto appeared.

"Where to?" he asked.

"There should be a big house just outside Mountain Hare in Wales."

"There is," said Umberto. "Grapeshot Hall."

"We need the mirror nearest the basement."

"OK," said Umberto.

"Right, listen," said Danny, while the mirror was whirring into its new shape. "While you go and get Roxie, I'm going to look for the Space

Twister."

"No way, Danny," said Mia. "Absolutely no way. We stick together."

"If we all rescue Roxie," said Danny, "we might not have time to get the remote. The Space Twister might have left by then."

Eric gave his Truth Spray another test squirt.

"Did you just aim that at me?" said Mia, turning round sharply.

"No, no," said Eric. "Just practising."

"If I ever catch you trying to spray me," said Mia, "I'll shove the whole bottle up your nose. And then – Danny? Danny?"

But Danny had already dived through the mirror and was now running as fast as he could along a dark corridor.

Danny twisted round and saw his sister looking out of the mirror on the long stone wall. But he didn't turn back. He'd made his decision and he knew she'd never agree with him. He had to get his remote back – fast.

Danny turned a corner and saw a concrete flight of stairs leading up to a green door. He climbed the stairs and edged the door open, peering through the crack. He could see a purple carpet, an ornate side table, a marble staircase. It must be the entrance hall, he thought.

He heard a man shouting. There was a tinkling noise, then a louder crash.

He couldn't work out what was going on, or whether the man was close by. He didn't know whether to keep moving or stay hidden.

Then he remembered his Time Tablet. He pulled it out and switched it on. The map of the world appeared. Danny clicked on the UK and then zoomed into Wales. He found Mountain Hare and clicked on it. There was a list of all of the streets in the town, and there, with a folder all to itself, was Grapeshot Hall. Danny grinned and clicked on it.

He would be able to see exactly who was in the house. He could read their file and work out what they were thinking and where they were going. He'd be able to move around unseen till he found his remote.

He looked at the names in the folder. There

was Roxie, Mia, Eric and himself.

That was it.

Impossible. He'd heard a man's voice, definitely a man's voice. He looked through the crack in the door again and saw the Space Twister. He had a long cane in one hand and a mobile phone in the other.

"You're sure you weren't drunk, Raymond?" said the Space Twister. "Or asleep? You didn't dream the whole thing?"

There was a mirror hanging above the side table. The Space Twister walked across to it and smashed it with the end of his cane.

"Then they must be using mirrors to move around," said the Space Twister into the phone. "It must be one of their infernal EUREKA! gadgets."

There was an oval mirror next to the front door. "Regency period, mahogany frame," said the Space Twister with a sigh. "I can't believe I'm doing this."

He smashed it to pieces.

"Listen, Raymond," he said, "you and

Terence will have to make your own way here. I need to think."

There were several mirrors on the far side of the hall. Danny watched as the Space Twister sauntered past them: smash, smash, smash.

Danny looked back down at the Time Tablet. Something was clearly wrong with it. The Space Twister's file should be inside the Grapeshot Hall folder. Danny wondered whether other people were in the house, too – hidden from the Time Tablet, invisible like the Space Twister.

It looked as if he'd have to find his remote without the Time Tablet's help.

He was about to step into the entrance hall when his legs felt suddenly heavy. Something was pulling his feet into the ground. A distant memory leapt into his head. Once more, he remembered his duel with the Night Scientist, having to press Fast Forward when the Night Scientist pressed Rewind.

The Space Twister must be using the remote. Danny could feel time slowing to a stop. He remembered Grace Bingley and tried to fight it, tried to free himself from it. But then the sensation passed and life started again.

As he crept into the hallway and peered up the stairs, Danny could see what had happened. The Space Twister had pressed Pause while he smashed the other mirrors in the house.

Nearly every stair had broken glass on it. Danny crunched his way up the first six steps and craned his neck round. The landing was carpeted with shards of glass, too.

Danny knew he was being reckless, but he kept climbing the stairs, peering up, down and around.

He reached the landing and opened the first door he saw. It was a bedroom. There was broken glass on the carpet that the door pushed backwards as it opened. In the centre of the room, there was a four-poster bed that looked as if it had never been slept in. The next room was also a bedroom, then there was a study and a bathroom and a TV room.

Danny found another empty bedroom and sat down on a chair next to the window. There were two empty mirror frames next to him, with shattered glass underneath them. At the end of the room, opposite the bed, there was a large, brown mirror that hadn't been broken.

Danny felt certain that the Space Twister – and the remote – had gone.

He pulled out his Time Tablet and took a deep breath. He should go back down to the basement and join the others. They would probably have found Roxie by now.

He touched the Time Tablet's screen and quickly brought up the Grapeshot Hall folder again. He clicked on it, thinking that he'd open Mia or Eric's file and find out where they were.

But, according to the Time Tablet, there was only one person in Grapeshot Hall. Daniel Danger. Danny gave the tablet a gentle shake. It seemed to be completely broken. First the

Space Twister's file had gone, now no Eric, Mia or Roxie.

Blimey, he'd only had it about two hours!

He wondered if anyone else was still showing up in the Tablet, or if it was just him.

He went back to the home screen and pondered for a few seconds, his fingers hovering over the screen. Then he clicked the search box and typed in his uncle's name.

There he was. Charles Baker. So some people were missing, and some people weren't.

He decided to quickly read the last few pages of his uncle's file, to check that he was OK.

"Take the headphones off, Jasper," shouted Charlie. "I need to talk to you."

"Eh?" said Jasper, lifting the headphone off his left ear.

Charlie shot out another sky rope and hit a thick bank of cumulus clouds.

"We're going to check out the Andante Caves," said Charlie.

"What are you talking about?" said Jasper. "They're in the Himalayas. Even higher than we are now."

"I know, I'm going to have to swing us above the clouds," said Uncle Charlie.

There was a pause. "You're funny," said Jasper.

"Don't worry, it'll work," said Charlie. "And, anyway, what other choice do we have? We've looked everywhere else. Now, Danny, I hope you're still reading. After you've visited Grace Bingley, go to Bambridge House in Dorset. It's a stately home; its owner has hidden EUREKA! agents in the past. I'll meet you there once I've found a crystal. We can talk about what Grace told you. You don't have to remember everything, we'll be able to read it all on your Time Tablet. Most importantly, stay with Roxie. You, Eric and Mia must never be alone. The Space Twister won't think twice about striking you dead if you're in his way. He's spared you once, Danny. He won't spare you again."

Uncle Charlie looked up at the next cloud and then continued to talk.

"I repeat: stick together. DON'T try and find your remote. And DON'T approach the Space Twister. OK, Jasper, I'm pulling us above the clouds NOW..."

and ... eat ...

... Hello! ... retired retired ...

scampi ... Leamington Spa ... Roman noses ... the ... the ... the ...

Danny stared at the screen for a couple of seconds. The Time Tablet was clearly broken. There were a few more lines of gibberish, and then all the text vanished from the screen and a pop-up box declared: "File not found."

Danny slid the Time Tablet into the back of his trousers and then looked out of the window.

His uncle needn't have worried. Danny wasn't about to approach the Space Twister. The Space Twister was probably halfway to America, or Australia, or Mars by now.

Danny thought about something else that his uncle had said: "You don't have to remember everything, we'll be able to read it all on your Time Tablet."

Danny looked back into the room. He'd just had an idea. He realised that he could read about Grace Bingley's early life on his Time Tablet. He could work out how she had twisted space. He could figure out how she had dropped out of time. He could imitate what she had done, beat the Space Twister and get his remote back. Unless his Time Tablet really was broken.

He'd get it out again and check.

Danny stood up and reached for the Time Tablet, but then sat back down again. He felt time slow down. He looked up and saw the Space Twister standing by the unbroken mirror at the end of the room.

"Danny Danger? You came for this?" he said, holding up the remote.

Danny stood absolutely still, fear in his eyes.

"It's nice to see you again. You know, last time you came after the remote, you got much closer. I had to rewind so much time."

"W-what do you mean?" said Danny, his voice trembling with terror.

"I mean, you actually had the remote in your hand. This is some time ago now, of course. It was all the fault of your uncle, and the robot that he gave your sister. Your little friend hacked into its factory settings and reprogrammed it so it could shoot multi-directional lasers. One of my ears was quite badly singed. Anyway, it was all very upsetting and I didn't wish to repeat the experience. So I had to get the remote back, then press Rewind all the way to the moment that your uncle's parcel arrived. I sent my men in and the parcel was pulverised. And then, sadly, I had to start all over again."

"W-what do you mean, start again?" asked Danny, his voice still shaking.

"Well, at that point, I'd only robbed one or two banks. Bought three houses. And most importantly, I'd only just started my antiques' collection. All of my vases, all of my jewellery – rewound back to the shops. I had to start my collection from scratch. All because of **you**!" The Space Twister was holding his face right up to Danny's.

"If only I could kill you, but alas I can't," said the Space Twister. "Your blasted uncle again. All EUREKA! devices are tied to their owners. If the owner dies, the device shuts down. So inconvenient."

The Space Twister took a step forward;

Danny backed away.

"The one person on Earth that I'd most like to kill is the one person on Earth that I have to keep alive…"

At this, the Space Twister smiled a bitter smile and all the jewels in his mouth sparkled. He grabbed Danny's chin and twisted it up and round.

"Talking of life and death, it's interesting you should choose now to make your latest attempt to get the remote back," said the Space Twister, "because I'm so close to a breakthrough, Daniel. So close. There's a museum in New Delhi that almost certainly contains the artifact that I've spent my whole life looking for."

"What artifact?" said Danny, trying to pull his chin away from the Space Twister's tight grip. "You've got the remote. What else do you need?"

The Space Twister chuckled. "You think this is about your useless gadget?" he said. "True, when I first stole it, I thought it would be the answer to all my prayers. I could pause time. I would never grow old. And if I did grow old, I could rewind myself and become young again. And so I had a happy few years, stealing money and generally having fun. But then I looked in the mirror. Were those grey hairs? And crow's feet? Because the remote doesn't stop us ageing, Danny. Time is rewound, but we are not. The remote removes us from time, but not from time's effects."

At that moment, Daniel forced himself to look more steadily at the Space Twister's face. He recoiled in disbelief and horror. Danny suddenly realised why the Space Twister looked slightly different each time he appeared.

The Space Twister must have been pressing Pause for weeks at a time. He must have rewound years and years and lived them back again.

He had been a young man earlier in the day when he had first taken the remote. Now his eyes were bloodshot, his neck was wrinkled, he had brown spots on his temples. He looked twenty or thirty years older.

"If you ever get the remote back, which I doubt," said the Space Twister, "then the same will happen to you. You see, every time you press Pause, time stops for your family and your friends. But it carries on for you. You're probably already a few months older than them. Soon, it will be a year. Two years. Ten years."

The Space Twister leaned back and looked at Danny. "So you see, Danny, the remote is useless. That is why I now spend my days looking for a very different gadget. Something that can make me forever young. Something that heals all scars."

Danny looked at the deep scar that ran down the Space Twister's face and tried not to shudder. "So – so," he stammered, "if you think the remote is useless, just give it back to me."

The Space Twister sighed. "Haven't you been listening?" he said. "I think I've found the artifact, the one that brings eternal life. But I can hardly steal it without the remote, can I?"

"But you can twist space. You can pause time whenever you like. What do you need the remote for?"

"Ah yes," said the Space Twister with a grin. The crystals in his teeth glittered more brightly than ever. "I was forgetting about that. You know, Daniel, perhaps I should tell you the truth about my space-twisting. I tell you what, if you join me, if you accompany me on my quest, then I will reveal everything. You too will twist space. You too will live forever."

Danny gazed into the Space Twister's burning eyes, one bright blue, one dark brown.

"N-no way," said Danny. "How could we ever be friends? You haven't twisted time, it's twisted you!"

The Space Twister took a step backwards. "Well, there's no need to be rude," he said. "Ah well, never mind. I thought you of all people might understand why I wish to escape my life."

He glanced at the time on the cosmic remote.

"Your friends should be here in about ten seconds," he said.

"My f-friends?" stammered Danny.

"Yes, they'll be coming through this mirror here. It's the only one left in the house. They've rescued that odd young woman in the basement. Now they think they're rescuing you."

The Space Twister tapped the mirror with the end of his cane. "I've never particularly liked this one. 1930s. Mock Tudor. I shall rather enjoy smashing it, to be honest."

"No!" shouted Danny at the top of his voice.

Roxie, Mia and Eric leapt through the mirror. Roxie was holding her catapult. "Come on, Danny," she said. "We've got to go."

The Space Twister swung his cane and the mirror shattered into thousands of pieces. "My dear girl," he said, "none of you are going anywhere."

Roxie spun round and pulled back the elastic on her catapult.

The Space Twister smiled and arched one of his eyebrows. He pressed Pause.

6
SLEEP

Danny blinked. Before he had closed his eyes, he had been standing on a wooden floor, staring at the Space Twister's pale, scarred face. When he opened his eyes, he was lying on his back in total darkness.

He put his hand down on the ground beside him. It felt like a rug or carpet.

He sat up and put his other hand out. He felt an arm. The arm didn't move. Danny took a deep breath and squeezed it.

He heard Eric's voice saying, "It can't be time to get up yet."

"Eric," Danny hissed. "Eric."

"Five minutes more," said Eric.

"It's not night time," said Danny. "It wasn't

a dream."

"Danny, is that you?" said another voice. It sounded like Mia.

"Mia? Where are you?" asked Danny.

"Over here," said Mia's voice.

Danny put his hand out.

"Ow, that's my eye," said Mia.

Mia's hand shot out.

"That's my ear you're twisting," said Danny.

"I can't see, I can't see!" exclaimed Eric. "Oh merciful heaven, please don't let me be blind!"

"What are you talking about?" said Mia. "The lights are off, that's all."

"Yeah, er, I knew that," stammered Eric. "I was, er, joking. Just keeping everyone's spirits up."

"Kids, are you OK?" said another voice.

"Roxie!" exclaimed Mia and Eric.

"Just be quiet till I get the lights on," said Roxie. "Who knows what's in here with us?"

This idea made Danny, Eric and Mia stop talking immediately. There were a couple of minutes of silence.

"Can you stop breathing, Eric?" whispered Mia. "It's really noisy."

"Only if you stop grinding your teeth," said Eric. "It's freaking me out."

There was a **crash** and a *roar*. Danny, Mia and Eric gave a yelp of fear and clung on to each other tightly.

"Sorry," Roxie whispered. "That was me. Knocked over a chair or something. Look, does anyone have a torch or a light source?"

Danny, Eric and Mia all patted their pockets.

"Hey," said Danny, fumbling with his trousers, "I've still got the Time Tablet. That'll give off some light."

He turned it on and a solid beam of light cut through the darkness of the room. It shone on a wall of books. Danny swivelled the tablet round and it lit up a sink, a hob and a fridge. He tilted it to the left and saw shelves of cans, tins and jars.

"Hold it there, I can see a light switch," said Roxie.

She released a pellet from her catapult, hit the switch, and three striplights flickered on, flooding the room with bright, white light.

"What is this place?" said Eric, his eyes wide.

The room was enormous. On the left-hand side, there was a kind of living room with bookshelves and a large sofa and a flat-screen TV. In front of them, there was a kitchen area, with tins of food stacked up on open shelves. To the right were six bunk beds, fully made up. Behind them, there was a lift and a wall full of buttons and gauges.

"OK," said Roxie, "he could have done us in, but instead he's put us here. Why?"

Eric ran over to the kitchen and grabbed a bag of peanuts from a shelf. "Honey roasted. Brilliant," he said.

"He's left us our gadgets too," said Danny. "Mia, do you still have your Mirror Key?"

Mia felt in her pocket and nodded.

Roxie looked down at her catapult. "Yeah, that is a bit freaky," she said. Then she looked up at the ceiling and across at the lift. "Unless he knows we'll never get out of here," she said.

She pointed her catapult straight up and released a pellet. It sank into the ceiling.

"Looks like titanium-tungsten. Strongest material known to man. Must be at least a metre thick," she said.

She aimed another pellet at the far wall. Again, it didn't bounce off, but sank in and stopped.

"Walls are even thicker," she said. "I've just realised what this place is. A bunker. A nuclear bunker. A lot of these old mansion houses have them. Built in the 1960s when everyone thought the Third World War was about to start. We're probably about two hundred metres below the ground."

Danny and Mia looked at each other.

Eric ambled over with a mouth full of peanuts. He threw a bag of crisps at Danny and one at Mia.

"Cheer up, folks," he said. "They've got chocolate raisins."

Danny quietly explained that they were in a nuclear bunker hundreds of metres underground.

"Seriously?" exclaimed Eric. "I've always wanted to go down in one of these!"

He ran over to the wall full of gauges.

"Wow, this must be where you monitor conditions on the surface. You know, see if it's safe to come out. This blue one measures radioactivity. This red one measures temperature."

He tripped across to the lift.

"And this must be the way back to the surface."

He pressed a Call Lift button. It fell off the wall.

"Right. Yes. I see. Hmm."

He picked up the phone that was mounted on the wall next to the lift. He listened for a couple of seconds, then put it down again.

"Oh," he said.

There were a few moments of silence.

"This is all your fault, Danny," said Mia. "I said we should stick together, but oh no, you had to go and get your remote."

"You should have stuck with me!" said Danny. "We should have got the remote first."

"Look, kids, since we're going to have to live here FOREVER," said Roxie, "let's try and be friends."

Danny took a deep breath and stared at his feet. Mia was right. It was his fault. He shouldn't have gone off on his own. He shouldn't have tried to take on the Space Twister. He should have listened to Uncle Charlie. He should have stuck with Roxie and rescued her first.

"Sorry, Mia," said Danny. "You're completely right. I should have listened. I've messed everything up."

"Yeah," said his sister, folding her arms. "You have."

"It's just – I thought the Time Tablet would help me get the remote," said Danny. "I'd be able to see where everyone was. But then it broke. The Space Twister wasn't in it. Then you weren't in it. Then Uncle Charlie wasn't in it. It all went wrong."

"What do you mean, I wasn't in it?" said Mia.

"You weren't in Grapeshot Hall," said Danny. "Your file just vanished."

"We went back to the cave to get Roxie's catapult," said Mia. "We must have been about five minutes. We wouldn't have been in Grapeshot Hall during that time."

"Oh," said Danny, "that makes sense. But what about Uncle Charlie? And the Space Twister?"

Mia shrugged. "What does it matter now? Your Time Tablet may as well be broken. We're trapped in a nuclear bunker. I cannot believe this is STILL my birthday."

Eric had been looking at the radiation gauge.

Roxie had been inspecting the lift doors. Now they both came over to join Danny and Mia.

"So why's he keeping us alive?" said Eric. "Why aren't we six feet under?"

"I don't think we're a threat to him any more," said Danny.

"What do you mean?" said Roxie.

"He told me that he's found something that will make him live forever," said Danny.

"What else did he say?" Roxie shot back. "Think, Danny. This could be really important."

Danny took a deep breath. He had been trying to forget his confrontation with the Space Twister. He didn't want to remember those cruel eyes, that sinister voice. Very slowly, Danny explained that the Space Twister had wanted the remote to make him stop time forever but it hadn't, he'd kept getting older, so now he was looking for something that could make him young again.

"This is bad," said Roxie. "If he has the remote and something that stops him dying, then he'll be – unbeatable – all-powerful."

She leapt over the back of the sofa and switched on the TV. A news reporter was standing at the end of a suburban street. He spoke in an urgent, staccato voice: "Shock scenes in Delhi today when the Indian National Museum announced that it had mislaid every item in its collection."

More headlines appeared across the bottom of the screen:

MUSEUM OF ANDALUCIA SAYS ANCIENT VASES ARE MISSING

ARIZONA MUSEUM OF NATURAL HISTORY LOSES NATIVE AMERICAN JEWELLERY

"It doesn't make sense, Danny," said Mia. "I thought you said he had some evil plan to live forever."

"Looks like he's just collecting more antiques," said Eric.

"Those aren't just antiques," said Roxie.

"What do you mean?" asked Danny.

"Every culture has a story about an object or garment that can make its owner immortal," she said. "You drink from the Holy Grail, you wear a phoenix's feather, you live for ever. All those museums he's looting. It can't be a coincidence. Each one of them contains their culture's most prized relic. The one that's supposed to grant you eternal life. We've got to get out of here before he finds the right one."

"You mean, there's a right one?" asked Eric, looking astonished.

Roxie pursed her lips. "Probably shouldn't have said that. Look, it's top secret, OK? Nobody outside of EUREKA! knows about it. I can't say anything more."

Quick as a flash, Eric pulled out his Truth Spray and squirted it at Roxie.

"Dammit, that's not fair," said Roxie.

"Course it is," said Eric. "Now, what are you talking about?"

Roxie clamped her mouth tightly shut and shook her head, but the words eventually burst out: "There's an amulet, made seven hundred

years ago by the medieval German craftsman Thelonius Grebe. It was meant to be presented to King Caracas of Velubia on his eightieth birthday, but the king died two days before the amulet was finished."

"So what does it do?" asked Mia.

"Anyway who wears it round their neck is immortal," said Roxie.

"Just like that?" asked Danny.

"We think so," said Roxie, "but we're not sure. There may be a trigger. Something that you need to do before its energy is released."

"So where is it?" asked Danny.

Roxie shrugged. "Nobody knows. It went missing on the day that Thelonius Grebe himself died. All we've got to go on is a riddle that he sent to the Queen of Velubia: 'My face is gold, my case is gold. For gold keeps out the wind and cold'."

Mia, Eric and Danny repeated the riddle to themselves.

"That could be anything," said Mia. "I've got a gold filling, he's welcome to that."

"My uncle's got a Labrador called Cindy," said

Eric. "She's got a gold face."

"Exactly, it's hard to work out what it means," said Roxie, "but it sounds like the Space Twister has heard rumours about the amulet. And, given he can pause time, he's likely to find it. We'd better get to it before he does."

"Great," said Eric, "as if we didn't have enough on our plate."

"I think we should start in Hamburg," said Roxie. "That was Grebe's hometown. Hamburg is bound to give us some leads."

"And how do you know this amulet works?" asked Mia.

But the spray had worn out and Roxie was shaking her head. She pulled out her catapult. "Save your spray for the bad guys, Eric. Unless you want a face full of pellets."

Eric put the Truth Spray back in his pocket.

"The less you know about the amulet, the safer you'll all be," said Roxie.

"So all we've got to do," said Mia, "is get out of here, find out where this amulet is, go and fetch the amulet, track down the Space Twister, get the cosmic remote back and put the Space Twister somewhere he can't make any more trouble."

Roxie nodded. "So let's start by getting ourselves out of here," she said, putting her hands on her hips and staring at the lift.

7

CUT AND PASTE

Roxie sprinted over to the lift and ran her finger along the join where the doors met.

"Stand back," she said.

She fired her catapult continually for at least a minute, aiming for the dead centre of the lift, but the pellets just bounced off.

"Try standing here," said Eric, pointing at a spot a few metres to the left of Roxie.

Roxie looked over her shoulder.

"You'll be at a fifty-five degree angle," Eric added, "and if your pellet reaches one hundred and twenty miles per hour, it should cause a chain reaction in the molecular structure of the right-hand door."

"For real?" Roxie asked.

Eric shrugged. "Think so."

Roxie did what Eric suggested, the pellet hit the centre of the lift with an ear-splitting clang, and the doors hissed open.

"You beauty!" exclaimed Roxie, running over to the open doors.

"Blimey, Eric, how did you work that out?" asked Danny.

"Granville's Eighth Law of Base Metals," mumbled Eric, with a shrug. "I thought everyone knew about it."

Roxie was peering into an empty lift shaft. She twisted her head round and looked straight upwards. "I can just about see the bottom of the lift. I'll try to get it down here," she said.

She glanced at the control panel next to the lift. She pulled open the radiation monitor and yanked out several metres of wire and cabling. She put one end of the cable into the sling of her catapult and leant into the lift shaft.

She fired the cable straight up the shaft, aiming at the lift.

The top of the cable wrapped itself around

a metal strut on the bottom of the lift; the rest of the cable dangled down into the shaft. Roxie started to climb.

She was about to disappear from view when she looked back into the bunker and said, "Mia, see if you can find any mirrors in here, any reflective surface, anything your Mirror Key will open."

She looked at Danny and Eric. "Use the Time Tablet to find out anything about the Space Twister's plans. Whether he's close to the amulet. And also – work out why Jasper hasn't flippin' beamed us out of here yet."

She pulled herself up the cable and out of sight.

Mia looked at Danny and Eric and said, "Let's go." She started going through drawers and cupboards, looking for even the smallest mirror.

Danny and Eric sat side by side on the sofa and turned on the Time Tablet.

"Who shall we look up first?" asked Eric.

"Uncle Charlie," said Danny.

He typed in Uncle Charlie's name and this time the Time Tablet found his uncle's file. But it still seemed to have a bug or glitch.

mackerel ... hold your horses ...
up down up up ...

Charlie and Jasper were back underneath the clouds.

"So the crystal wasn't there either," said Jasper with a sigh.

"There's one last place we can try," said Charlie.

"You know what, we should have kept the Time Tablet. Then we could have just typed in the original inventor's name and found out everything he knew."

Charlie fired another sky rope into a long bank of clouds. "No way," he said. "Danny needed it far more than us. Besides, you know that it wouldn't work. It's programmed to respond to Danny's thumbprint."

"That's true. I forgot," said Jasper.

"Every EUREKA! agent gets just one gadget," said Charlie, "but lucky Danny gets two. Because in fact the cosmic remote and the Time Tablet are two halves of one gadget. The control panel and the hard drive. That's why one fingerprint controls both."

"I remember now," said Jasper.

"Every time someone uses the cosmic remote, it searches the contents of the Time Tablet," said Charlie, "that's how it knows what to rewind, what to pause. Hang on, we're going above the clouds again..."

Charlie fired a sky rope into the highest cloud in the sky.

"Danny, if you're reading this ... remember what I said about ... hide ... wait at the ... find you ... find you ...

tea cosy ... decathalon ...

Danny frowned. "It did that before," he said. "Stupid thing."

But Eric was only half listening. "I get it," he mumbled. "The cosmic remote moves time, but the Time Tablet tells it what to move. They're linked. The cosmic remote is the car, but the Time Tablet is the sat nav."

"Eric, what are you talking about now?" asked Danny.

"When you press Rewind or Pause, the remote checks the Time Tablet and finds out what people are doing. What they've done. It's the remote's brain. So what if we hack into its brain!"

"I still don't get it," said Danny.

"Well, at the moment, you can only read the Time Tablet," said Eric, "but what if you could write into it, too? What if you could change everyone's files? We'd soon get out of here. We'd soon beat that Space Twister bloke."

"Hang on," said Danny. "Say that again."

Eric repeated what he'd just said.

"You're serious?" asked Danny. "That's possible?"

"It must be," said Eric. "Every system can be breached. Remember when I hacked into the school website and changed all the teachers' names to Shirley Ollerinshaw?"

Danny nodded and then a light went on in his eyes.

"Hang on, Eric," he said. "The Space Twister told me that, when we nearly beat him before, it was because you took that robot that Mia got for her birthday and hacked into it. Made it shoot lasers."

"Wow," said Eric. "I did that?"

"Yeah, you did," said Danny. "So you should definitely try hacking again."

"Not a problem," said Eric, rubbing his hands together. "Let's find the back door. Every programmer always puts in a back door. Click there. Now double click there."

Danny looked at his Time Tablet and did what Eric said.

Mia was crawling under the bunk beds now, still looking for a mirror.

"No, not there," said Eric. "Go back, go back. Bring up the map again. Now zoom into there."

Danny clicked and zoomed.

"That's it!" exclaimed Eric. "That small island: St Zoombia. It can't be real. Zoombia's a game for the B-FORCE 250. The developer must have created it specially. That'll be the way into the program settings."

Danny clicked on the island. A box full of icons filled the screen.

"Now tick the box that says administrator,"

said Eric.

Danny ticked the box.

"Click the button that says Save settings," said Eric.

Danny clicked the button.

"And we're in," said Eric.

He clapped his hands. Mia looked up from a chest of drawers and walked over to her brother and Eric. "What have you done now?" she asked.

"Open someone's file," said Eric. "Actually, open mine."

Danny typed in Eric's name and brought up his file.

"Now click on it and look," said Eric. "There's a menu of options. You can Cut, Paste, Edit, Delete. Move people round. Change their lives."

"Danny, hang on," said Mia. "This is serious stuff. Just hold on a minute."

"You can get us out of here!" said Eric enthusiastically. "Don't worry, I'll go first. Just click on my file and select Cut. Then navigate to my house. And paste me there."

"Eric, don't be a nut," said Mia.

"It'll be fine," said Eric. "It'll just be treating me like a block of code. Safer than a flippin' plane or your uncle's sky ropes, that's for sure. Come on, click Cut. I'll vanish for a bit, but that's what's meant to happen."

"Eric, shouldn't we try this on someone else first? Someone we don't like?" asked Danny.

"No way," said Eric. "I hacked into it, I go first. Come on, Danny, I want to go home."

"Don't do it, Danny," said Mia. "You can't trust that fruitcake."

Danny looked at Eric. "Maybe not, but it's his choice," he said.

He gritted his teeth and clicked Cut.

Eric vanished from the bunker.

"Oh no, oh no," stammered Mia. "What have you done?" She ran over to the lift shaft and called out, "Roxie! Roxie!"

Danny was concentrating on the Time Tablet. He was going to do exactly what Eric said. He found the file for Eric's house, opened it and clicked Paste.

Eric's file appeared next to **GEORGE TAYLOR** and **LUCY TAYLOR**. Danny opened the file and quickly scrolled to the end. It read:

Eric materialised in the middle of his room.

"Woah, that was seriously weird," he said. "It's like I've just come off a roller coaster."

Eric looked down at the floor.

"Oh no, I landed on my mp3 player," he said, lifting up one of his feet.

"He's OK!" said Danny. "It worked!"Mia was peering over Danny's shoulder. "This can't be possible," she said. More words appeared at the end of Eric's file, one letter at a time.

"You know what, Danny," said Eric. "This would be a

good time to see if Edit works. See, you should be able to change people's files."

He picked up a twisted piece of plastic from the floor.

"Just select Edit and then click into the end of my file and type 'Eric found a brand-new mp3 player under his bed'."

"What's he talking about?" said Mia.

"Eric said you could edit people's lives," said Danny. "You can type new sentences into them."

Danny clicked on Eric's file and chose Edit. Then he clicked after the last sentence in Eric's file and a cursor appeared.

"Oh my…" stammered Danny.

"I don't believe it," said Mia.

Danny typed:

Eric found a brand-new mp3 player under his bed.

There was a brief pause and then the Time Tablet took over. Two sentences quickly appeared.

Eric picked up the mp3 player and grinned.

"Thanks, Danny," said Eric. "I could use some new headphones, though. I trod on them as well."

Danny looked at Mia in wonder. Then he typed:

Eric picked up a pair of headphones from the bed.

There was a pause and then more words started to shoot across the screen.

He plugged the headphones into his mp3 player.

"Brilliant," said Eric. "Now you'd better get yourselves out of there, too. Cut and paste just like you did with me. See you in here in a few minutes."

He started to press the buttons on his new mp3 player.

"This is a Hansen G75," said Eric. "Nice one, Danny."

Danny closed Eric's file.

"I can't believe it actually worked," said Danny. "I teleported Eric. I typed something into his file and it actually happened."

"You're like a Greek god or something," said Mia.

"If only the Space Twister was in the Time Tablet, I could just type 'He dropped the cosmic remote down the toilet' and it would all be over," said Danny quietly.

"OK, look," said Mia. "Let's just wait for Roxie before we do anything else. Who knows what you actually just did?"

"No way," said Danny. "I'm getting us out of here. It's my fault that we all ended up in this bunker. I'm going to put it right."

"No, hang on…"

"I'll paste you out, then Roxie, then me," said Danny. "Then we can all go and find the Space Twister together."

"It just feels dodgy," said Mia.

"It's fine," said Danny, "but look, if you want me to go next… "

"No, no, OK, OK," said Mia. "I'll go next. If it goes wrong, then I'll get vaporised, not you."

Danny gave a short nod.

He typed in Mia Danger and found his sister's file. He clicked on it and selected Cut. Mia didn't disappear.

"You sure you got the right Mia Danger?" asked Mia.

Danny looked again at the Time Tablet.

"Whoops," he said. "Wrong one. She looks about ninety."

"Guess you should put her back then," said Mia.

"I could put her back somewhere else," suggested Danny. "You know, somewhere nice. Give her a holiday."

"Like where?"

"I don't know," said Danny. "Disneyworld?"

"She's ninety," said Mia. "She's not going to like Disneyworld."

"All right, Frinton, then," said Danny. "The dinner ladies at school are always going on about Frinton."

Suddenly there was a loud clunk that echoed around the bunker. There was an even louder whirring noise and a deafening metallic squeal.

Danny and Mia twisted round. The lift had started to move.

"Roxie must have got it working," said Mia.

"OK, let's give her a surprise," said Danny. "When she gets back down, it will just be me in here."

Mia gave a half-smile and nodded.

Danny quickly pasted the wrong Mia Danger back where she was and found the right Mia Danger.

"Ready?" he asked.

"Think so," said Mia, trying to look braver than she felt. "Actually, I've changed my mind."

"OK," said Danny, looking up from the Tablet.

"No, no," said Mia. "It's fine. Do it. Do it."

Danny clicked Cut and Mia was gone. It was odd, but Danny felt more troubled by his sister vanishing than when Eric had disappeared. His fingers started to quiver and, for a moment, he couldn't move his hands. He felt hugely relieved when he clicked Paste and saw Mia's file appear next to Eric's. He opened his sister's file and read:

Mia appeared in Eric's room next to Eric. She

ran over to the window and threw up on to the grass below.

She pulled her head back in and exclaimed: "That was unbelievable! Danny, you've got to try this!"

Back in the bunker, the lift hummed and clanked.

At that moment, a strange thought crossed Danny's mind: what if it wasn't Roxie in the lift?

As quickly as he could, he found Roxie's file in the Time Tablet and scrolled to the last few paragraphs:

Roxie was standing in the middle of the lift with a thug on either side of her. Her hands were tied behind her back so she couldn't reach the catapult that sat in her front pocket.

"Are we going to break her legs, Steve?" said the first thug.

"Maybe one leg," the second thug replied. "She *is* a lady."

There was no time to lose. He had to cut and paste Roxie out of there. Roxie wouldn't understand what was happening, but she was in EUREKA!, she'd assume it was Jasper, or Uncle Charlie, or a new gadget.

Danny was about to paste Roxie into the same folder as Eric and Mia, but then he remembered what she'd said about the magical amulet. She'd wanted to find it before the Space Twister. She'd wanted to start her search in Hamburg, the inventor's home town. So Danny found Hamburg on the map, clicked on the Town Hall folder and pasted Roxie there.

Then he clicked on the first thug, selected Cut, clicked on the Sahara desert and pasted him next to a sand dune. He pasted the second thug on to a tiny island in the middle of the Caspian Sea.

The lift was slowing down.

Danny whispered: "It's my turn. Time to cut and paste myself."

He found his own folder and clicked on it. There were the options: Cut, Paste, Edit, Delete.

He was about to select Cut, when his chest tightened.

Where do I go when I click Cut? he thought. *Does the Time Tablet come with me? Surely it can't. So how do I click Paste? I won't be able to, I'll be cut forever.*

A split second later, the empty lift appeared in front of him with a loud ping.

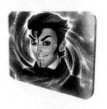

8
EDIT

Danny stepped into the lift. It was large and modern with a floor-to-ceiling mirror on the back wall and a handrail that ran along all three sides.

There were only two buttons: Bunker and Ground. Danny pressed Ground. The lift started to whirr and move upwards.

Danny would have to find another way out of Grapeshot Hall. He could cut and paste other people, but he didn't see how he could cut and paste himself. Or, at least, he could cut himself, but then there'd be nobody left to paste him.

He'd just have to leave in the normal way, through the front door.

But, Danny thought, *it will be fine*. He held

his Time Tablet in front of him. He had found the Grapeshot Hall folder. If anyone got in his way, he would click Cut and Paste and dump them in the Amazon jungle.

As the lift doors opened, he looked down at the Time Tablet's screen. There were five people in the house: **DANIEL DANGER, BARRY MCINTYRE, STEVE JARROW, RONNIE COLLINS** and **DUDLEY RIX.**

Danny looked at the images on top of the folder icons. The other four men looked like the Space Twister's thugs.

He stepped out of the lift and almost stepped back in again. He had never seen so many beautiful objects in his life. The room was only four metres wide and six metres long. But everywhere Danny looked, there were Greek vases and Roman plates, Viking tankards and Egyptian dishes. There were chairs and tables stacked up to the ceiling; wardrobes on top of wardrobes and rugs heaped up on cabinets. On every surface, jewellery glittered. There were bracelets and necklaces and rings and brooches and tiaras and anklets and crowns.

Danny was about to
cross the room when
he heard a scuffling
noise in the corner.
He turned round but
couldn't see anyone or
anything. Slowly,
a shape emerged
from behind a
chest of drawers.
It was an old man
wearing a long black
cloak. He was staring
at a necklace in his right
hand, unaware of Danny's
presence.

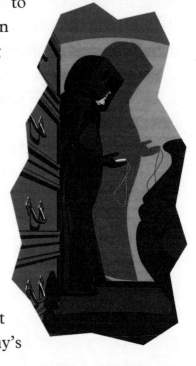

Danny glanced down at his Time Tablet. He
looked at the four names in the Grapeshot Hall
folder beside his own. He wondered who this
was.

The old man shuffled towards Danny and
then looked up in surprise.

"Good heavens," he said. "What are you doing in here?"

Danny almost dropped his Time Tablet. His face was contorted with fear.

The old man was the Space Twister. At least seventy now, his hair was white, his cheeks were sunken and his scar blended in with the other deep wrinkles and lines on his face. Only the jewels in his teeth were unchanged.

"Of course," said the Space Twister. "I'd put you down in the bunker, hadn't I? And now you've broken out."

Danny suddenly remembered his earlier encounter with the Space Twister. He hadn't been able to see him in the Time Tablet. The Space Twister's file hadn't been there.

His file still wasn't there. Which meant that Danny couldn't cut or paste the Space Twister. His Time Tablet was no use to him.

The Space Twister, however, still had the remote. He had pulled it out of a pocket in his cloak.

"Now, should I rewind you back to the bunker

or should I let you watch my transformation?" said the Space Twister, tapping the remote on his cheek.

"I think you should watch," he decided, "because this is what I offered to share with you."

He put the amulet around his neck. "This is the object I've spent fifteen years searching for," the Space Twister announced. "'Its face is gold, its case is gold,' goes the riddle. Perhaps you're familiar with it?"

Danny tried not to react.

"Anyway, this is twenty-four carat," continued the Space Twister. "The purest gold there is. Now watch me become young again."

He threw his head back and closed his eyes. Danny watched, still frightened, wondering whether he should run away while the Space Twister wasn't looking at him. But he stayed where he was: he had to see what the Space Twister's amulet would do.

A few seconds passed. The Space Twister remained standing, his head thrown back, his arms flung out. Danny looked at his face: it was still lined and wrinkled.

The Space Twister stood with his eyes closed for a few more seconds, then started to pat his face. "I don't believe it!" he exclaimed. "It's the wrong amulet! It's the wrong amulet AGAIN!"

Danny couldn't help smiling. He felt suddenly confident and stared at the remote in the Space Twister's hand. He was about to pounce, when the Space Twister's eyes met his.

"Oh no, you don't," said the Space Twister. "Looks like I'll be needing your gadget for a little while longer. Back to the bunker with you. Barry! Steven!"

Danny took a step backwards, still staring at the remote. If he could just take it back here and now, then everything would return to normal.

He heard the door to the room being flung open and remembered his Time Tablet. Part of him thought he should keep it hidden, stop the Space Twister from seeing it. But another part of him wanted to fight back. Now he could cut and paste and edit, his Time Tablet was surely more than a match for the cosmic remote.

Four thugs were standing behind the Space Twister.

"Take him down to the bunker," said the Space Twister, pointing at Danny, "and this time, make sure he doesn't escape. Ever."

Danny dived underneath a pile of chairs and wriggled into a cabinet. He left the door open so he could still see the room in front of him. As one of the thugs waddled towards the pile of chairs, Danny glanced down at his Time Tablet. He found the first thug's file, clicked Cut and the thug vanished.

The other three thugs turned round and looked at the space where the missing thug used to be.

"Dudley's run away again," said one.

Danny pasted the thug on top of the Empire State Building in New York.

The Space Twister shrieked, "Get him! He's just a child, for heaven's sake!"

Danny decided to try editing again. He chose the thug that was closest to him, found his file and clicked on it. He chose Edit and a cursor appeared at the end of the last sentence in the thug's file. Danny quickly typed:

The thug was chased by a bear.

The text on the screen immediately changed to:

The thug turned round. He thought he heard a bear, but he was mistaken.

OK, Danny thought to himself, *it has to be something that could happen. Or the Time Tablet rejects it.*

He typed:

The thug jumped out of the window.

Danny craned his neck and watched the thug run across the room and jump out of the nearest window. There was a loud shattering noise as glass flew everywhere.

The other two thugs ran over to the empty window frame and peered out.

"He's this way, Barry," one of them shouted.

A distant voice groaned: "Not – sure – why – I – did – that."

Danny clicked on another thug's file. He chose Edit and typed:

The thug climbed up the chimney.

The thug that had shouted out of the window turned round, strode across the room, pushed aside a table and pulled himself through the mantelpiece.

The thug who was left behind peered up the chimney and said: "Is this one of your clever plans, Steve? Are we luring him on to the roof?"

"How are you doing this, young man?" the Space Twister drawled, staring at Danny through the stack of chairs.

Danny ignored him and clicked on the last thug's file and typed:

He lay down on the floor and fell asleep.

The remaining thug yawned, stretched and collapsed in a heap on the floor.

The Space Twister looked round at the thug and then back at Danny. "OK, time to press Pause and stop this nonsense."

Danny's mind was racing. He needed to get the remote out of the Space Twister's hand, but the Space Twister's file was still not in the Time Tablet. He glanced quickly round the room and saw that the Space Twister was standing directly under a large crystal chandelier.

The Space Twister was pointing the remote at Danny. Danny opened his own file and typed:

The chandelier fell on to the floor and knocked the Space Twister out.

There was an almighty crash as the chandelier shattered on the floor. But, at the last second, the Space Twister leapt out of the way. Danny typed:

A wardrobe started to totter and fell on top of the Space Twister.

The wardrobe next to the door gave way and began to fall forward. The Space Twister glanced over his shoulder and jumped sideways. The wardrobe hit the floor with a thunk.

"How is this happening?" exclaimed the Space Twister. "Is this some new EUREKA! gadget?"

Danny couldn't believe the Space Twister was still standing up. Without being able to type into the Space Twister's file, Danny seemed to have less control over what happened to him.

Then Danny noticed the thug that was asleep on the floor. An idea flashed into his head and he clicked into the thug's file. He selected Edit and started to type:

The thug woke up and picked up an old book from a

large pile on the floor. He walked across to where the Space Twister was standing and whacked him on the head with the book. Then he handed the cosmic remote to Danny.

The Space Twister was about to press Pause, when Danny said, "Look who's just woken up."

The Space Twister watched as the thug stood up and picked up a dictionary from a pile of books on the floor.

Danny continued to type:

After handing Danny the remote, the thug biffed himself in the chops and knocked himself out.

The Space Twister stood up and faced the thug. "Barry, put the book down, you can't even read."

The thug lumbered across the room.

"Barry, whatever he's doing to you, you can fight it."

The thug stared at the Space Twister with confusion in his eyes.

"Barry, he's doing this with some silly gadget," said the Space Twister. "You work for me, remember. You follow my orders."

"Sorry, boss," mumbled the thug and whacked the Space Twister with the book. The Space Twister dropped to his knees.

The thug took the remote and walked across to the pile of chairs. He shoved them out of the way and gave the remote to Danny. Then he heaved a deep sigh and knocked himself out. Danny looked at the remote. He couldn't believe his eyes. It was over. He felt light-headed with relief and delight.

He clambered out of the cabinet and stood in the middle of the room. He saw that the Space Twister and the knocked-out thug were starting to stir, so he pressed Pause. Everything froze. Now Danny felt even safer, even happier.

OK, he thought to himself. *What next?* Roxie was in Hamburg, Eric and Mia were in Eric's house, Uncle Charlie and Jasper were in mid-air. He needed to tell everyone that he had the remote and the crisis was over. Perhaps the easiest thing to do was just rewind the whole day and start again. Only this time, the Space

Twister wouldn't get anywhere near his remote.

He jammed his finger down on rewind and watched the thug that was knocked out walk backwards across the room. Another thug tumbled out of the chimney and another leapt into the window backwards.

The Space Twister didn't move. He stayed where he was. Then, very slowly, he stood up.

Danny let go of Rewind and stared at the Space Twister in terror. He pressed Pause.

The thugs all froze but the Space Twister kept walking towards him.

"I'm not a bad person," said the Space Twister, rubbing the back of his head.

Danny leant against a table, barely able to stand.

"I could have killed off your friends, but I didn't," said the Space Twister. "I didn't have to tell you about the magical amulet, but I did. And this is how you respond to my kindness."

Danny was backing away, moving towards the lift doors. He looked down at the remote. He had pressed Pause, the time was saying: 13:05:55, 13:05:55.

"This is impossible," said Danny.

"Of course it's possible," said the Space Twister. "When are you going to realise: The. Remote. Doesn't. Work. On. Me."

The Space Twister was centimetres away from Danny. "It doesn't matter how many times you take it," he said. "I'll always take it back."

The Space Twister snatched the remote out of Danny's hand.

Danny felt wretched, terrified, powerless. "H-how are you doing this?" he stammered. "Are you l-like Grace Bingley?"

"Oh, no, no, no," said the Space Twister. "It was when I visited Grace Bingley that I realised space-twisting wasn't for me. I saw that twisting space removes you from time, but not from the ageing process. Do you know how old Grace is? Sixty-eight. At least, sixty-eight of our years. Over a hundred for her."

Danny murmured in confusion.

"Shame I didn't realise that before my own experiments with time," said the Space Twister, touching his scar. "They cost me my good looks. But anyway. The moment I left Grace's house, I started to pin all of my hopes on your remote. Your useless. Pathetic. Remote."

"So- so," said Danny, "how are you im-imune from it?"

The Space Twister shook his head. "Time's up, Danny. I've got an amulet to find." He grinned and the crystals in his mouth glistened. He yanked off the amulet that hung round his neck, tossing it on to the floor.

Danny stared at the Space Twister, at his white, haggard face and the sparkling crystals in his teeth. Then something clicked in Danny's mind. He looked again at the jewels in the Space Twister's front teeth. He quickly looked away, trying to process what he had seen.

The Space Twister pressed Play. He leaned across Danny and touched the "Call Lift" button on the wall. Behind the Space Twister, the thugs were looking around with dazed expressions.

The lift was already on the ground floor and the doors pinged open. The Space Twister shoved Danny backwards. Danny staggered into the lift and leaned against the mirror on the back wall.

The Space Twister leaned in and pressed the "B" button. "This time, you'll never get out of the bunker, Danny," he said. "You'll stay there forever. And while you're down there, I'll be sending Barry and Steven around the world. They'll be rounding up your friends and family and killing them all. You've committed the worst possible crime against me. You've wasted my time. My precious time."

He stared darkly at Danny, looking older than ever. Danny wanted to reach for his Time Tablet, but his hands refused to move.

The Space Twister turned round and faced the four thugs. "Kill his sister first. Then his best friend. Bring me their heads on spikes."

"N-no," mumbled Danny.

At that precise moment, two heads popped out of the mirror on the back wall of the lift. One was Eric's and one was Mia's.

"If he comes near my head, I'll nut him," said Mia.

The lift doors began to close. The Space Twister saw Eric and Mia and wedged his foot in the lift doors.

"Damnation!" he exclaimed. He jammed his finger on the Pause button of the remote.

Eric and Mia grabbed Danny by the shoulders

and dragged him into the mirror. Mia locked the mirror behind them and looked down at Danny. "This is positively the last time we rescue you," she said. "Ever."

9
DELETE

Danny looked up and around at the small grey room. He was behind the mirror in the lift, safe from the Space Twister.

He stood up and hugged Mia. He was about to hug Eric then he stopped.

"All right, mate?" said Eric.

"All right, mate?" Danny replied.

"What are you both doing here?" asked Danny.

"We couldn't leave you in there, could we?" said Mia. "We came through the mirror in Eric's downstairs toilet."

"Listen, listen," said Danny, suddenly remembering, "I've worked out how he's twisting space. It's the jewels in his teeth. I saw it. I saw it!"

"Saw what?" asked Mia.

"One of them is an amber crystal," said Danny.

"What?" said Eric.

"He's got an amber crystal in his teeth," said Danny. "He can't twist space. He doesn't even want to, because it doesn't stop you ageing. So he's doing something else. With the crystal."

"You mean, like he's become a remote himself?" asked Eric.

"He can't have done, or he wouldn't need Danny's, would he?" said Mia.

"All right, it was just a theory," said Eric.

"I've got a theory," said Mia. "You and Danny are doing my head in."

"Be quiet for a minute, I'm trying to think," said Danny.

He opened his Time Tablet and typed in "BARRY MCINTYRE". It was the name of one of the Space Twister's thugs.

"We've got to find out what's going on," said Danny.

They all read the end of Barry McIntyre's file.

The Space Twister and Barry were standing in the lift with the doors wedged open.

"I don't understand it," the Space Twister exclaimed. "I pressed Rewind and they didn't come back out of the mirror."

"If you say so, boss," replied Barry.

"Wherever they've gone, they must be outside of time. Not in range." The Space Twister looked down at the remote.

"So do you still want me to chase them or not, boss?" asked Barry.

"Yes, yes," said the Space Twister. "Actually, no, it doesn't matter. The amulet is more important. This must be the wrong one. If only I could find out who wrote that riddle. Maybe the author was also the inventor."

"Wow, so we're immune from the remote in here," said Eric.

"That is pretty handy," said Mia.

"Yeah," said Danny, nodding. "Let's keep reading. And start writing."

He selected Edit and typed,

"So what happened back there, boss? Did the kid take your remote?"

There was a pause and then a sentence scrambled across the Time Tablet.

"Not that it's any of your business, Barry," replied the Space Twister, "but yes."

Danny typed,

"So how did you get it back, boss?"

There was another pause and then the following words appeared.

The Space Twister looked at Barry suspiciously and said, "It's not like you to exhibit curiosity, Barry. But, since you ask, I'm immune from the gadget's powers because of this crystal in my front tooth."

Danny continued to type, making the thug ask more and more questions.

Mia and Eric read:

"Good one, boss," laughed Barry. "But, seriously,

how did you do it?"

"I'm quite serious," replied the Space Twister. "This crystal is the same as the one used by the gadget." He held up the cosmic remote. "It tricks the remote into thinking that I am also a cosmic remote."

"So why do you need the gadget, boss?"

"Because I am a cosmic remote without controls," said the Space Twister. "The crystal in my teeth means that if someone else uses the remote, I do not get paused or rewound or fast forwarded. But if I want to control when time pauses or gets rewound, I can't. Hence needing the remote too."

"Blimey, boss, how did you work that out?"

The Space Twister narrowed his eyes and looked at Barry. "I must admit, it's quite nice to talk to someone about all of this. But you don't seem yourself, Barry. Are you sure you're ALL THERE?"

Danny stopped typing and looked at Eric and Mia.

"He's twigged," whispered Eric.

Danny, Eric and Mia watched more words appeared on the Time Tablet. Danny wasn't controlling Barry any more.

"Eh, boss?" said Barry.

"Those questions you asked," said the Space Twister.

"What questions would they be, boss?" asked Barry.

"Just as I suspected," said the Space Twister. He looked up at the ceiling. "I don't know how you're doing this, EUREKA! But the fun's over."

He pulled out the cosmic remote.

"I've just had an idea," said Eric. "Danny, keep him talking."

Danny nodded and started to type into Barry's file, taking over his body again.

"The fun's just started," said Barry. "You're finished, Space Twister. Or whatever your name is. It's hardly right to call you the Space Twister when you can't even twist space."

The Space Twister's reply appeared on the Time Tablet.

"I'm not saying another word," said the Space Twister. "I'm pausing time. Good day."

While Danny had been typing, Eric had been talking to Mia. "Very quietly, open the mirror at the back of the lift again. Just for a few seconds."

"Why?" Mia replied.

"Just do it," said Eric.

Mia unlocked the mirror and Eric took out his Truth Spray. He put the nozzle through the mirror and very gently squirted it for about twenty seconds.

"Close it, close it!" said Eric.

Mia locked the mirror.

Eric leapt over to where Danny was standing and said, "That room will be full of Truth Spray now. They can't lie."

"Cool," said Danny. "Let's work out the whole story."

He started to type again, continuing to use Barry as a puppet.

"So how did you find the crystal?" Barry asked.

The Space Twister clamped his lips together but the words came tumbling out. "It was a stroke of luck, really. After I visited Grace Bingley, I gave up twisting space. I looked into other ways of controlling time. I found an article about time travel in an obscure scientific journal called FAST FORWARD. The writer was Herbert Perkins or, if you prefer, the Night Scientist. He'd been eighteen or nineteen when he wrote it, but twenty years had passed. So what had happened to him? It took me two days and two nights to track him down. When I arrived at his laboratory complex, it was empty except for a broken cosmic remote on the floor of an abandoned warehouse. There was an amber crystal next to it. I had no idea what it was, but I put the crystal in my teeth for safekeeping. Shortly afterwards, I noticed time stopping and going backwards."

"What do you mean, boss?"

Again, the Space Twister tried not to speak and again, the words came out in a torrent. "Well, the boy Danny Danger was clearly using his remote. The crystal in my tooth meant that I wasn't affected by it. The first time it happened, I had no idea what was going on. I thought I was space-twisting without realising it. But then time resumed again in the normal way. After a few weeks of research, I worked out why."

"So now you've got the remote, why are you still wearing the crystal?" asked Barry.

"Because of what just happened in here," the Space

Twister replied. "The boy took the remote back. For a few seconds only. But it meant that, when he pressed Pause, I was immune from it. So I could take it back."

"So without the crystal, you can be paused as well," said Barry.

"Yes," replied the Space Twister. "I'll be just as... What am I saying? Why have I said all this?"

He was staring at his mouth angrily.

"It's run out," said Eric.

"Open the mirror again, Mia," said Danny. "I've worked out how to finish this."

"What do you mean?" said Mia, running back to the mirror and unlocking it.

"We'll get the crystal out of his teeth first," said Danny. "Then the remote. Then we can all go home."

"You're not going out there," said Mia, standing in front of the mirror.

Danny shook his head. "No, it's coming in here."

He typed as quickly as he could:

Barry held the Space Twister down and pulled the

amber crystal out of his teeth. Then he threw the crystal into the mirror at the back of the lift.

A split second later, an amber crystal flew into the small grey room.

Danny typed:

Barry took the cosmic remote from the Space Twister.

He was about to type "Barry threw the remote into the mirror", when a message appeared on the screen: "New folder has appeared in Grapeshot Hall. Do you want to view?"

Without thinking, Danny clicked Yes.

And there, next to Barry McIntyre's file, was the new addition. He saw a picture of the Space Twister on top of a small yellow folder icon.

Of course, thought Danny. *Without the crystal in his teeth, he's just like anybody else. He's in the Time Tablet. I can do whatever I want to him.*

"Danny," exclaimed Mia. "Why hasn't the remote come through the mirror?"

Danny had clicked on the Space Twister's folder. He looked at the options. Cut, Paste,

Edit, Delete. For the first time, he stared at the Delete option.

Delete. Destroy. Remove forever.

He could delete the Space Twister.

"Danny, why aren't you typing?" asked Eric.

Danny selected Delete. A message appeared on screen.

Deleting will remove this person from time forever. Are you sure?

"Danny, I'm not keeping this mirror unlocked for much longer!" cried Mia.

Danny stared at the two options. Delete or Cancel. It would all be over. He just had to delete the Space Twister.

A few seconds passed.

He couldn't do it. He just couldn't. He was about to click Cancel when the Space Twister's file vanished. He quickly clicked into the first thug's file again and read:

"Give that back, Barry!" shouted the Space Twister.

Barry looked lost. "Give what back, boss?"

"The remote in your hand," said the Space Twister.

Barry glanced down at his hand. "Oh, right. Sorry, boss."

The Space Twister snatched the remote and pressed Pause. He vanished from the room.

Mia had locked the mirror and was standing in front of Danny. "What happened?" she said.

"He got away," said Danny.

"How come?" said Eric.

"H-his folder appeared and I thought I c-could delete him and—" Danny mumbled.

"*Delete* him – woah," said Mia, taking a step backwards.

"It just appeared as one of the options and I thought – *it'll solve everything. He'll be gone for good.* But I didn't. I couldn't."

"Thank goodness for that," said Mia. "If you'd killed him, I'd have – er – well – killed you."

"But his folder was in there, right?" said Eric. "So that means we can find him again. We can still stop him. You just have to type in his name."

Danny looked ahead blankly. "I didn't really

take in his name," he said quietly.

"What?" cried Mia.

"I just saw his folder and clicked on it, I didn't really notice what it was called," said Danny.

"You ... didn't ... notice...?" said Mia. "Danny, how could you be so daft!"

"Hey, calm down," said Eric. "It'll still be OK. After all, we got the amber crystal. Which means that, you know, if we had the remote, the Space Twister wouldn't be immune from it any more. But since we haven't got the remote, the crystal's, er, a bit rubbish really."

Danny stared at his feet. It was the third time in a single day that he had failed to get his remote back. Maybe he should just find his own file and delete himself. Do everyone a favour.

"Hang on a sec," said Eric. "Last time we checked, wasn't your uncle flying through the air, looking for a crystal? Didn't he say he could build another remote with it?"

Mia stopped frowning and said, "Actually, yeah, he did say that."

"So that's what we should do," said Eric. "Find your uncle."

There were a few moments of silence.

Mia looked at the crystal and then looked at her brother. She nudged Danny and said, "Forget the Space Twister. Let's find Uncle Charlie and give him an early birthday present. Even though I'm still waiting for MY present from him."

Danny was still looking at the floor, but managed the smallest of smiles.

10
ENTER

Mia, Danny and Eric were in the small grey room, staring at the Time Tablet's screen. Danny had opened up his uncle's file and they were all reading it.

zbc

bimpoopbim

..." have to look for the crystal later..."

"OK, let's spilt up, then," said Uncle Charlie, firing a sky rope into a thick bank of cumulus clouds.

"Where do you think they are?" asked Jasper.

"I don't know," said Uncle Charlie, "but I told them to meet me at Bambridge House. You know, where we've hidden before. Danny would have read it on his Time Tablet. And they weren't there. So something's happened."

Danny winced. He'd completely forgotten about his uncle's instructions. Danny read on, praying that his actions hadn't brought about more disaster.

"OK, well, I'm going to Germany first," said Jasper, taking a small black phone out of his pocket. "I just got a missed call from a phone box in Hamburg. Answer phone message is Y.O.U. S.U.C.K., tapped out on the receiver in Morse Code. Can only be Roxie, right?"

"I'm going to find the Space Twister's headquarters," said Uncle Charlie. "He might have captured Danny. Or Danny might have gone there himself. Hunting for his remote."

"Really? You think he'd be that reckless?"

Uncle Charlie nodded. "I'd have done the same."

Uncle Charlie and Jasper swooped down and, when Uncle Charlie got close to a row of skyscrapers, he said, "The outskirts of Hamburg. Shall I drop you on the top of one of those buildings?"

Jasper nodded. "See you back at the skylab."

"If you see the Space Twister," said Uncle Charlie, "run or hide. Until we've found a crystal."

Uncle Charlie swung close to the skyscraper and

dropped Jasper down a giant air-conditioning chute. Then he swung round and headed north. He pulled a notepad out of his pocket.

"Space Twister has three known hideouts. Let's start with Grapeshot Hall."

Charlie raced through the sky at huge speed, shooting one sky rope after another. Within five minutes, he was lowering himself on to the roof of Grapeshot Hall and flipping open a skylight.

He went from room to room, looking for Danny, Eric or Mia, but found no trace of them. Then he heard raised voices coming from behind a small door at the end of the library. He ran across to open it, but time was suddenly paused and he froze.

Danny was the first to finish reading it. "Oh no! Uncle Charlie's out there!" he exclaimed.

Mia and Eric finished and looked up.

"Do you think the Space Twister saw him?" asked Mia.

"It doesn't look like it," said Eric. "I mean, your uncle's still in the Time Tablet, isn't he? Just paused."

"But we're not leaving him out there," said Danny. "What if the Space Twister comes back? Or presses Play and all those thugs come back to life?"

"So what are you saying?" asked Eric.

"I'm going out there to get him!"

"Right, and what about if the Space Twister presses Play and the thugs come back to life and you're out there," said Eric.

"Mia, unlock the mirror, please," said Danny.

"Or what if he presses Play and Pause and then you're frozen too," said Eric.

"Mia, please, it's my fault Uncle Charlie's out there," said Danny. "Unlock the mirror."

"Or what if he presses Rewind and you're

out there and we're in here," said Eric. "Who knows where you'll end up?"

"Mia, I've got the Time Tablet," said Danny. "If anything happens, I can cut and paste people. I can even … delete them, remember."

Mia was listening to all this, holding the Mirror Key in her right hand and patting her left hand with it.

"You'll never be able to carry him through here on your own," said Mia.

"I can," said Danny. "I will."

"Either we all go or none of us goes," said Mia. "We are sticking together from now on."

"Exactly," said Eric. "Thank you."

"So we all go," said Mia.

"Exactly," said Eric. "We all – hang on a minute. What did you say?"

Mia unlocked the mirror. "We'll only be out there for thirty seconds, Eric," she said. "He's standing just behind the door."

"Yes, a door with a big sign on it saying DEATH TRAP," said Eric.

"OK, let's leave my uncle out there to get

pulled apart," said Mia. "Do you want that on your conscience?"

"I won't have a conscience if I'm dead, will I?" grumbled Eric.

Danny and Mia put their heads through the mirror. After a few seconds, Eric reluctantly joined them.

The lift doors were still wedged open and they could see part of the room in front of them. A thug was standing behind a chair, paused. He was staring straight ahead of him, looking confused. Two other thugs could be seen, frozen next to a window. One was halfway through a yawn and a bit of dribble had just dropped off his bottom lip.

"Flipping heck," said Mia. "So this is what it looks like."

"Did I mention that I think this is a bad idea?" said Eric, looking around the room in wonder.

"Every time you paused the world, this is what happened," said Mia.

Danny nodded.

"Come on, let's go," he said.

He stepped out of the mirror and walked across the room. As he passed the first thug, he shivered. He didn't think he'd feel any fear, but he did. Although he'd paused the world dozens of times, he'd always been controlling it. He'd had his remote. This was different.

Mia stopped by the first thug and prodded him in the stomach. Her finger folded back on itself. "It's like he's made of rock," she said.

"Let's keep moving," said Danny. As he crossed the room, he gazed down at his Time Tablet. He opened the Grapeshot Hall folder and looked at the files inside. There was his uncle's file, there were all the thugs. He was ready to strike if he needed to.

Eric had pulled out his Truth Spray. "You've got my back, right, Danny?" said Eric. "And, Mia, you've got my back too, right? Cos you look like you've got each other's backs but not my back. It's very important that someone gets my back."

There was a tinkling noise and all three of

them spun round, terrified.

"Sorry," said Eric, nodding at the glass jar he had knocked over.

Danny opened the door of the room and saw his uncle floating about half a metre off the ground. It looked as if he had just thrown himself at the door, on the point of breaking it open.

Danny couldn't help smiling; he was so relieved to see his uncle again, even if he was frozen stiff.

"Come on," said Danny. He tucked his Time Tablet into the back of his trousers and grabbed one of his uncle's legs.

Eric and Mia grabbed Charlie's other leg.

"Right, this is how it works," said Danny.

"First we have to wrench him out of time. That's the hardest bit. After that, it's easier."

They pulled Uncle Charlie down towards the ground. He moved slightly, then sprang back up to his original position.

"That one moved, I swear he moved," said Eric, pointing at one of the thugs by the window. Because of his position, the thug happened to be staring straight at them.

"Try again," said Danny. "I've managed this on my own before. One more yank should be enough."

"OK, on three," said Mia. "One, two, threeeee."

They all pulled and Uncle Charlie landed with a thump and toppled forward, hitting the floor with his face.

"Good job he couldn't feel that," said Eric.

"Come on, let's pick him up," said Danny.

Mia and Eric nodded and grabbed his shoulders. "Wow, now he weighs next to nothing," said Mia.

"Weird, isn't it?" said Danny.

Eric was glancing at the thugs, looking for the slightest movement. They got Charlie into the lift and were about to drag him through the mirror.

"What happens now?" said Eric.

"What do you mean?" asked Danny.

"I mean, when we drag him through the mirror, does he stay frozen? How do we unfreeze him?"

At that moment, Uncle Charlie became as heavy as rock. They struggled to hold him. Eric was the first to let go, dropping one of Uncle Charlie's legs. This caused Danny and Mia to lose their grip too. Uncle Charlie hit the floor and opened his eyes. "Did I drink too much?" he asked, slightly dazed.

"You're awake!" said Danny. "But that means if you're awake—"

Time had started again in the cluttered room. The four thugs were looking at Eric, Mia and Danny with startled expressions. Then they pelted across the room.

"In the mirror, quick! Quick!" yelled Danny.

Uncle Charlie seemed to realise what was going on, picking up Eric and chucking him through the mirror. Danny and Mia leapt through and Uncle Charlie followed.

"Phew, that was cl—" said Uncle Charlie, as they landed in the small grey room. But he was being dragged back through the mirror: first his legs, then his waist.

Danny, Eric and Mia grabbed Uncle Charlie's arms and pulled as hard as they could.

"Keep pulling, don't let go," said Danny to Eric and Mia, whipping out his Time Tablet. There was no time to cut and paste them all individually. So he clicked on one of the thugs' files and typed: "The thugs all started to do chicken impressions."

Eric and Mia pulled Uncle Charlie back into the small, grey room.

"Ruddy hell, what just happened there?" Uncle Charlie looked down at his left leg. "I think one of them was trying to *peck* me."

"Uncle," said Mia, "we've got a lot of catching up to do."

11
RETURN

Danny, Eric and Mia told Uncle Charlie exactly what had happened over the past few hours.

Danny explained how they had gone to see Grace Bingley and how she could slow down time.

"Blimey," said Uncle Charlie.

Eric told Uncle Charlie that the Space Twister couldn't actually twist space, he just wore a crystal in his teeth to fool the remote.

"Crikey," said Uncle Charlie.

Danny explained that the Space Twister had used the remote to pause time for years and he was now incredibly old. He was looking for an amulet to make him young again.

"Flipping 'eck," said Uncle Charlie.

Then Mia said that they had hacked into Danny's Time Tablet and they could edit reality and change people's lives. "That's how we got this," she concluded, holding up the amber crystal.

Uncle Charlie stared at it in disbelief. "Incredible," he murmured and took it out of Mia's hand. "It's genuine too," he added, holding it up to the light.

"I know," said Mia. "Danny got one of the thugs to pull it straight out of the Space Twister's teeth."

At that moment, Danny was hit by a wave of self-pity. He said, "We'd have pasted the Space Twister into prison too if I hadn't got confused and messed everything up."

"Hany on, hang on," said Uncle Charlie. "Nobody's messed anything up. You've all done amazing things. And now we've got this crystal, we can make our own remote and fight back."

Danny smiled at his uncle and felt much better.

"OK, we've got to get this to the skylab straightaway," said Uncle Charlie.

"The what lab?" asked Eric.

"EUREKA! owns a hot air balloon that floats above the clouds," said Uncle Charlie. "We only ever use it in emergencies. We might need to make a detour, though."

"What do you mean?" asked Mia.

"Well, you mentioned that the Space Twister is looking for an amulet," said Uncle Charlie. "I'm pretty sure that'll be Grebe's amulet."

"It is!" exclaimed Mia. "That's what Roxie called it!"

"Well, there's no way on earth we can let him get that. He'll be immortal. Free to do anything, anywhere, forever and ever. We'll need to pick that up first."

"You mean you know where it is?" asked Danny.

"Roughly," said Uncle Charlie.

"But Roxie's gone looking for it," said Danny.

"That's why she's not here with us. I pasted her to Hamburg. She said she wanted to look for the amulet there."

"OK, makes sense," said Uncle Charlie. "Jasper thought Roxie had called him from Germany. But Grebe's amulet ain't in Hamburg. Still, it's OK. Jasper's gone to fetch Roxie. We'll all meet up in the skylab."

Uncle Charlie looked again at the crystal in his palm. "Pulled it out of his teeth," he said with a chuckle, shaking his head.

Then he looked up at the children again.

"OK, let's think about how we do this," said Uncle Charlie. "It's still dangerous out there. I can't risk any of you getting paused. If what you said is true, the Space Twister will murder you on sight."

"Well, we're safe in here," Eric told him.

"What do you mean?" asked Uncle Charlie.

So Eric explained how when they were behind a mirror, they were immune from the remote.

"Of course, you're outside of time," said

Uncle Charlie.

"We drop out of the Time Tablet too," said Danny.

"Of course you do," said Uncle Charlie, nodding. "The remote can only control people in the Time Tablet. So maybe you three should stop here where he can't touch you."

"Cool!" exclaimed Eric.

But Danny remembered something else.

"The Space Twister wasn't in the Time Tablet when *he* was wearing the crystal," said Danny.

"Yep, makes sense," said Uncle Charlie.

"And *you* weren't in the Time Tablet either, when you swung really high. The words just became gibberish."

"Of course!" exclaimed Uncle Charlie.

"Or your file vanished," said Danny.

"Brilliant!" said Uncle Charlie.

"At first, I thought the Time Tablet was broken," said Danny, "but maybe—"

"There's no maybe about it," said Uncle Charlie. "When me and Jasper were above the clouds, we were out of range. The remote and the Time Tablet are only designed to work on Earth. And when we're above the clouds, it thinks we've left Earth. This keeps getting better. When we reach the skylab, we'll be immune from the remote."

Uncle Charlie's face shone with satisfaction.

"OK," said Eric, "but didn't you say we had to pick up the amulet too?"

"That'll almost certainly be at a high altitude as well," said Uncle Charlie. "It won't count as Earth either."

"Er … where is it, then?" asked Mia.

"Best if I explain on the journey," said Uncle Charlie. "Let's get going. Mia, use your Mirror Key to find us somewhere with lots of clouds. Somewhere I can use my sky rope to swing us up very high very fast."

Mia nodded and started to talk to Umberto.

"I could try cutting and pasting you, Uncle," suggested Danny, pulling out his Time Tablet. "I can put you anywhere you like."

"Some other time," said Uncle Charlie.

"Much as I love the sound of it, it would mean leaving you behind, right? Who would cut and paste you? Also, nothing above the clouds will be in your Time Tablet. Not on Earth, remember. So you couldn't paste me to the skylab."

Uncle Charlie joined Mia over by the mirror. They kept peering out and inspecting the sky in different countries.

Danny looked down at his Time Tablet. It was strange to think that the Space Twister was in here now, if only he could find him, if only he knew his name. Then Danny began to think about how all of these amazing gadgets had drawbacks or flaws. None of them had been able to stop the Space Twister yet.

This led him to think about Grace Bingley again. She had natural power, natural ability. If he could twist space like her, he wouldn't need any gadgets. The Space Twister could have remotes and amulets and Mirror Keys, but Danny could twist away from all of them.

He opened Grace's file and began to skim

through it. One passage near the beginning jumped out immediately:

Grace first realised she could slow down time one day at school.

It was playtime and the bell rang. Grace didn't want playtime to end so she found herself listening to the bell. She focused on the ringing noise, making it slower and slower in her head. The sound of the bell got lower and lower until it was just a slow rasp, then a sludgy rumble. Then the noise stopped and life stopped and Grace walked slowly through a playground full of mysterious statues.

Danny murmured, "How do you slow down a sound?"

Then his uncle called out, "Danny, we're all set!"

Danny was back in the present. He joined Mia and Eric and Uncle Charlie by the mirror on the wall.

"OK," said Uncle Charlie. "We're at the Derwent Water Visitor Centre. Loads of cumulonimbus clouds. We should be able to leave Earth fast. Stick close together and tell me if you see anything – ANYTHING – weird."

"What about Eric's face?" suggested Mia.

"What about Mia's brain?" retorted Eric.

"Come on, you love each other really," said Uncle Charlie, and Mia blushed and Eric mumbled something inaudible.

Then Uncle Charlie said, "Right, we're moving out."

12
ZOOM OUT

Eric, Mia and Uncle Charlie walked through the mirror. Danny tucked his Time Tablet into the back of his trousers and followed them.

They were standing outside the Derwent Water Visitor Centre. The mirror was propped up against the side of the building, ready to be moved to its new home in the disabled toilet.

"Quick as you can," said Uncle Charlie, and led the children down a slope into open ground.

They had only been outside thirty seconds, when Danny felt the bottom dropping out of his stomach. He felt his feet sinking into the ground and his arms going limp. He knew what was happening: the Space Twister was pressing Pause. He had felt it when he had fought the Night Scientist, he had felt it earlier this morning at Grapeshot Hall. If he could feel it, then surely he could pull himself free of it? The words of Grace Bingley were still echoing in his head. He tried to focus on a sound, tried to slow it down, tried to make the sound deeper and longer. For a split second, he saw Mia turning round in slow motion.

Then a bolt of pain shot through the middle of his body, so intense that he opened his mouth in a silent scream, then he relaxed, the pain went away, and life started again.

"Uncle Charlie," Danny gasped. "Uncle Charlie!"

Uncle Charlie had pulled out his sky rope handles.

"The Space Twister just pressed Pause," said Danny.

"What do you mean?" Uncle Charlie replied, spinning round. "How do you know?"

So Danny explained how he could feel it when time was being paused.

"Danny," said Mia. "There's blood on

your head."

Danny put his hand up to his forehead and looked at his finger. There was a splotch of blood on it.

"What have you been doing?" she asked, narrowing her eyes angrily. "If you've been trying to twist space after what I—"

"No," lied Danny immediately. "I haven't, I haven't. I knocked my head on the mirror frame." He put his hand to his head again and felt a thin dent in the skin above his eyes.

"There's no time to argue with each other," said Uncle Charlie. "If the Space Twister pressed Pause, he could have killed us all. We can't risk that happening again."

Uncle Charlie aimed his sky rope at a nearby cloud. At the same moment, a spot of rain landed on his head. Uncle Charlie scowled at the sky. He ignored the rain and shot his sky rope directly upwards.

The sky rope travelled a few metres, then made a loud fizzing noise, gave off hundreds of bright red sparks, and then flopped on to the floor.

As Uncle Charlie retracted it, he said quickly, "Sky ropes aren't great when it rains. They're designed to lock on to water vapour."

More spots of rain were falling.

"The rain confuses its hydrotropic sensors," said Uncle Charlie. "We'll have to find clouds somewhere else. Come on, back to the mirror."

Danny felt his limbs locking and his stomach tightening. The world was being paused again. This time, he didn't try to fight it. He was still shaking slightly from his last attempt to twist out of time. The sensation quickly passed.

"Uncle," he gasped. "He pressed Pause again."

"Dammit," growled Uncle Charlie. "We can't stay out here." He looked wildly left and right. He couldn't decide whether to run back to the mirror or try his sky rope one more time.

Eric was staring at something in the sky. "Charlie," he said. "Did you say that your sky ropes lock on to any water-based moisture in the atmosphere?"

"Yep," said Uncle Charlie distractedly.

"Then that might be the quickest way out of here," said Eric, pointing up at the sky.

Uncle Charlie, Danny and Mia looked up and saw an aeroplane moving slowly into the clouds.

"Great idea!" exclaimed Uncle Charlie.

"Eric, what have you just suggested?" groaned Mia.

"I'll aim at one of the planes taking off from Manchester airport!" said Uncle Charlie. "Come on. Up here." He bounded back up the slope, followed by Danny, Eric and Mia. The rain was falling more steadily now.

"From this vantage point, I'll be able to fire at a thirty – or forty – degree angle," said Uncle Charlie. "That should cut sideways through the rain. Plus a plane's vapour trail is so dense that it will be an easy target."

He pointed his sky rope diagonally upwards.

"Climb on, kids," said Uncle Charlie, "and hold on tight. I mean, seriously tight."

A plane was nosing its way into the sky.

"Ahem, Charlie," said Eric, clearly having second thoughts. "Maybe we should have a test run first. Let's start by getting towed behind a milkfloat or a golf cart. Then *work up*."

"No time," said Uncle Charlie. "Next stop, the stratosphere."

Mia, Danny and Eric hesitated and looked at each other.

"Do you want to get paused? Maybe forever?" asked Uncle Charlie.

Mia, Danny and Eric clung on to Uncle Charlie: Mia on one arm, Danny on the other, Eric on Uncle Charlie's back.

Uncle Charlie shot one of his sky ropes into the white fumes that were pouring out of the back of the plane. At first nothing happened. The end of the sky rope vanished, lost in the haze. Charlie looked frustrated, as if the rain had foiled his plans again.

Then all four were snapped off the ground and flung sideways through the air in a vast arc.

They watched the grass and the lake and the visitor centre whip past beneath them. Suddenly the sky rope was pulled taut and they were yanked in directly behind the plane's engine. They were pulled upwards incredibly fast, riding the plane like they were water-skiers behind a flying, rocket-powered speedboat.

"Whaaaaaaa!" said Danny.

"Flipping-blooming-ruddy-blimey-stinking-ruddy-crikey," said Eric.

They couldn't really move or speak or see, the skin was pulled back so far on their faces as the plane went faster and faster.

Uncle Charlie held on as tightly as he could. The sky rope was shaking and jerking, trying to stabilise itself.

The aeroplane roared as it banked to the left.

"This is – complete-ly in-sane!" Mia screamed.

A split second later, they were above the clouds.

Uncle Charlie breathed a deep sigh of relief.

Danny and Mia gasped as the soft, fluffy carpets of clouds unfolded for miles on all sides.

"We just need to get a bit higher," said Uncle Charlie. "Hang on."

Another plane was flying in the opposite direction, pointing diagonally upwards. Uncle Charlie shot his other sky rope into its vapour trail. The four of them were sucked across the sky at vast speed, before the rope went taut and they were dragged along directly behind the second plane.

"And again," said Uncle Charlie, as he fired

a sky rope at a third plane that was climbing higher still.

This time, after they'd been pulled across the sky, Mia cried out, "Eric, were you just sick on me?"

"No," said Eric, slobbering slightly.

"This top is hand wash only, you know!"

"Probably someone flushed the loo on the plane," said Danny with a giggle.

Eric giggled too and quietly dabbed at the sick on his chin with his sleeve.

Uncle Charlie was looking up and frowning and looking down and scowling.

"OK, judging by the position of the Great Bear, we'll be above Mount Everest in two minutes," he shouted. "I'm going to retract my sky rope shortly before this. We'll drop gently into a snowdrift on the summit. It'll be a bit chilly, but we'll only stay a minute at the most."

"What?" exclaimed Mia.

"This cannot be happening," said Eric quietly, looking at the clouds below him and the stars above. "Five hours ago, I was at home, in my jimjams, eating porridge and watching *Pingu*."

"You know I said we had to stop off for the amulet?" continued Charlie. "Well, that's what we're doing. We'll grab it then head to the skylab."

"The amulet's on top of Mount Everest?" said Danny.

"Sort of," said Uncle Charlie. "Look, what I'm about to tell you is absolutely top secret. Only EUREKA! agents with Level One clearance are allowed to know this. That's me and Professor Larkspur, and she's been missing for nine months. So – basically – it's just me. Which means: you cannot breathe a word of what I'm about to tell you."

Danny, Eric and Mia nodded.

"Five hundred years ago," said Charlie, "when Thelonius Grebe first created the amulet, he wasn't sure if it would actually work. Could it really make anyone who wore it young forever? So he decided to test it on one of his pets. He hung it round the neck of a golden eagle that he'd brought home from an Oriental excursion. Grebe died shortly afterwards and all of his pets were released into the wild. Nobody realised that the amulet actually worked. And nobody realised that the eagle was still wearing the amulet. Which means that the eagle is *still* wearing the amulet..."

The aeroplane slowed down, preparing to descend.

There in front of them, Danny, Mia, Eric and Uncle Charlie saw the top of a mountain, peeking through the clouds. And, on a small ledge, just below the peak, they saw a small brown shape, shuffling from side to side and staring directly at them.

As they got closer, the shape grew more distinct.

"No way," murmured Mia.

"That's Grebe's eagle," said Uncle Charlie. "Right where I suspected it would be."

"How?" asked Eric. "How could anyone know that?"

"It's had five hundred years to find the

perfect roosting place," said Uncle Charlie. "Five hundred years to work out the safest place, the highest place, the most beautiful place. That's got to be at the top of the world's highest mountain."

"So hang on," said Danny. "That's what the riddle meant. What was it? 'My face is gold, my case is gold. For gold keeps out the wind and cold.' It was talking about a golden eagle, not something made of gold."

Uncle Charlie nodded. "Professor Larkspur and I cracked the riddle a year ago. Actually, it was mostly Professor Larkspur."

Danny was about to ask who Professor Larkspur was, when the mountain loomed up in front of them and the eagle came into focus. An amulet was visible on his chest, hanging from his neck on a silver chain. He was  staring regally into the distance.

"Hang on," said Mia. "If we take it off him, won't he die? If he's five hundred years old."

"No, no," said Uncle Charlie. "He'll just start to age at the normal pace. Besides, we'll only borrow it for a day or two, until the Space Twister is behind bars. Then he can have it back. So – all ready? I'm about the retract the sky rope."

Danny, Eric and Mia said, "Ready."

Uncle Charlie put his thumb on the sky rope. He was about to press it, when a thumping, thudding noise began to echo around the mountaintop. It got suddenly louder.

A helicopter swung out from behind the mountain. The Space Twister and one of his thugs were inside.

Uncle Charlie instinctively shot his sky rope sideways, hitting a heaped-up lump of dark cloud.

The helicopter lurched towards Uncle Charlie and the children, and its rotary blades chopped the sky rope in two.

Uncle Charlie and the children hurtled

downwards. Uncle Charlie quickly shot his other sky rope into another cloud and swung them round the other side of the mountain.

Danny fumbled for his Time Tablet, but it was no good, they were moving too quickly, he couldn't reach it.

Uncle Charlie retracted his broken sky rope, and then shot it out again. It was half the length, but still long enough to hit a bank of cumulus cloud a few hundred metres above their heads.

He swung them back round to where the eagle had been perching.

But the helicopter, and the eagle, and the amulet were gone.

13
SCROLL UP

The EUREKA! skylab floated slowly through the sky, about a hundred metres above the highest cirrus clouds. It was kept afloat by a giant balloon with alternating red, blue, yellow, brown, orange, green, violet, black and pink stripes. The skylab itself was a small airtight box with thick glass walls on all sides and a metal floor with a hatch in the middle of it. Against every wall, there were computers, machine parts, toolboxes, dog-eared manuals, chipboards and coiled-up cables.

Mia was pushed through the hatch in the floor, followed by Eric and Danny. Uncle Charlie climbed in after them. They all looked at each other for a few seconds.

"It's over, isn't it, Uncle?" cried Danny. "We'll never get the remote back now. He can do whatever he wants."

"If only we'd got there ten seconds before," said Mia. "Eric, you should have thought of your brilliant idea sooner. We could have caught an earlier plane."

"Yeah, well, if you hadn't slowed us down," replied Eric. "You're three years older and a lot heavier than me and Danny."

"Stop it, all of you!" growled Uncle Charlie, with a rare flash of anger. "It's my fault. No one else's. I keep underestimating the Space Twister. And now I have to put things right. By building a remote as quickly as I possibly can."

He pulled the amber crystal out of his pocket.

"I'm going to be working in this corner," said Uncle Charlie, pointing at a workbench with a blowtorch on it. "Danny, get that TV working, tune it into a news channel, try and find out what the Space Twister is up to. Eric, you should be able to get the Internet on that laptop. I need any extra information you can give me about amber crystals and the energy they contain. Mia, see that periscope? I need you to tell me whenever you see anything or anyone approaching us by air."

Danny, Eric and Mia all headed off to different parts of the skylab.

Danny switched on an ancient TV that was sitting on the floor under a trestle table. A black-and-white picture briefly appeared on the screen, then turned into grey snow and jagged lines. Danny spotted a white dial next to the screen, and turned it clockwise. Another picture came into focus, a character from an American soap opera.

Danny wondered if his Time Tablet would be more useful. But as soon as he switched it on, he remembered. Above the clouds, it would not work. He typed in his own name just to check. File not found.

He kept turning the dial on the TV until finally a news presenter stared back at him. He turned up the volume and listened.

"And now, back to our main story.

A mystery benefactor is about to open a brand-new museum in London, full of the greatest inventions in history. Exhibits will include the world's first computer, the world's largest robot and the world's fastest rocket. It will also have a games zone, where visitors can play every computer game ever made on one of two hundred special consoles. Another section will be full of classic theme-park rides like the MANGLER, the WHITE TIGER and BLAST OFF. Most amazingly of all, everything I just mentioned will be located in a giant glass dome, a hundred metres tall and three hundred metres in diameter."

There was video footage of people on ladders hanging banners on to a curved pane of glass.

The reporter went on: "The man who has set up this miraculous museum – seemingly overnight – is known only as Mister Twister. He has released this statement: 'For years, I have been collecting fascinating objects. But I have allowed nobody else to see them. It is time I gave something back. It is time I did something … for the children. This is why I have created the Science Palace.' "

Danny was staring at the screen in distress and disbelief. The Space Twister had built this amazing place? It made no sense at all.

The reporter concluded: "Admission to the Science Palace is one hundred pounds per person, but remember that one special group of people get in for nothing. That's right. If your first name is ERIC, then it won't cost you a penny."

There was footage of a small boy with a microphone in front of his face.

"What's your name, son?" a man off-screen was asking.

"Eric," said the boy.

"And how do you feel about getting into this new museum for free?"

"Makes sense," said the boy. "Eric's a great name, innit? They should let us in to Legoland free as well."

Danny turned the volume down and sat for a couple of minutes. He thought about what he had just seen, letting it sink in. He glanced across the skylab at Eric, typing away at the laptop. Perhaps it was just a coincidence that the Space Twister's latest venture involved people called Eric. Perhaps, but Danny still felt bewildered and frightened for his friend.

Danny flicked through a few different news channels to see if the Space Twister was hatching any more dastardly schemes. But no – the other news stories were normal enough. There were no strange pranks, no thefts from art galleries – just the giant glass museum with free entry for Erics.

Danny heard voices behind him and saw that Eric had crossed the skylab and was standing next to Uncle Charlie.

"So I've been reading about amber crystals," said Eric.

"Blast!" exclaimed Uncle Charlie as a screw pinged out of a chipboard.

"There's good news and there's bad news," said Eric.

"Drat!" shouted Uncle Charlie, as a rubber

Play button plopped on to the work bench.

"The bad news is that, according to the equation of crystal density divided by planet size, well, then, er, the crystal is too small," said Eric.

"What did you say?" said Uncle Charlie, looking up.

Eric repeated what he had said and explained his logic.

Uncle Charlie put his head in his hands. "You're right, you're right. Oh, this is disastrous. When we broke the Night Scientist's remote, we must have shattered the crystal. And the Night Scientist had already split the original crystal in half to make his own remote. The Space Twister only ever had a small fragment. So that's it. We're finished. We can't build a remote after all. Heaven help Planet Earth."

"Hang on, there *is* good news," said Eric.

Uncle Charlie shook his head. "No, no, there isn't."

"There is, there is. You see, there's nothing to stop us doing what the Space Twister did," said Eric. "The crystal's easily big enough to protect you, or me, or Danny or Mia. You just wear it in your teeth."

Uncle Charlie blinked.

"We become immune from the remote," said Eric. "Just like he was."

Uncle Charlie was still blinking. Then he turned to face the workbench. Very slowly, he picked up a small hammer that was lying next to a tangle of wires. He picked it up, swung it high and brought it down on the crystal as hard as he could.

"No!" exclaimed Eric. "What are you doing, what are you doing?"

Danny twisted round and took a step towards his uncle. There was an ear-splitting clang. The crystal shivered, cracked and split into three.

"It would have worked," said Eric, looking devastated. "The evidence was sound."

"I know," said Uncle Charlie slowly, "and it will still work."

"What do you mean?"

"As you said, the crystal was easily big enough to protect you," said Uncle Charlie. "In fact, it was three times too big."

Eric thought for a moment, frowned, opened his mouth, closed it, smiled and nodded.

"What are you talking about?" asked Danny.

Uncle Charlie picked up the three pieces of crystal. "There's one for Eric. One for Danny. And one for Mia. From now on, you wear these in your teeth all the time. Even if you're up here. Even if you're with me."

Danny and Eric took their crystals. Mia was still standing by the periscope that stuck out of the middle of the floor. She continued to stare into it, on the look out for the enemy.

"What about you?" said Eric to Uncle Charlie. "Don't you need one?"

"I'll be fine," said Uncle Charlie. "Jewellery doesn't suit me."

"But what about building a remote?" asked

Danny, staring at the crystal in his palm. "What about taking on the Space Twister?"

"I'll need to find another crystal for that," said Uncle Charlie. "Or think of another plan altogether."

"Well, you'd better hurry up," said Danny, "because the Space Twister is already up to something pretty strange."

"Strange?" repeated Uncle Charlie.

Uncle Charlie and Eric joined Danny by the TV.

Danny turned up the volume and stood back from the screen. There was more footage of the Science Palace. After a few minutes, Eric said, "I can't ruddy cruddy believe I'm going to miss that!"

"Don't be daft, Eric," said Danny. "You can't trust the Space Twister."

"Look, Danny," said Eric. "Just because it sounds like a trap, and looks like a trap, and feels like a trap, doesn't mean it *is* a trap."

"Is he trying to get the crystal back?" Uncle Charlie muttered, thinking out loud. "But why? He's got the amulet. Or is he trying to manipulate time again? But how?"

"I've got a great idea!" exclaimed Eric. "You let me go down and check it out. I'll have the crystal in my teeth so he can't hurt me. Come on! Did you see? Metal Gretel, the world's biggest robot, is going to be there!"

"No way, Eric!" said Danny. "This whole thing – the Science Palace – the people called Eric – it's just—"

"If you're worried, we can all go together," said Eric. "All wearing our crystals. And if the Space Twister does leap out, you can have one of your showdowns – you know, a bit of chatting, a bit of fighting – and get your remote back this time. That way, everyone gets what they want."

"OK," said Uncle Charlie slowly, "maybe the best thing to do *is* to visit the Science Palace."

"Yes!" exclaimed Eric.

"What?" said Danny.

"But not till Roxie's here," added Uncle Charlie. "We're going to need her help."

"Bums," groaned Eric. "She could be on her way to Mars. She could be locked inside a maximum security prison."

"Uncle Charlie," Mia called out, looking up from the periscope.

"What is it?" said Uncle Charlie, spinning round.

"You know you told me I should stay on look out. Just in case anyone tries to get up here?" said Mia.

"Yes," said Uncle Charlie.

"Well, it looks like we have a visitor."

Uncle Charlie strode across the skylab and stood next to the periscope.

"And I think it's Roxie," said Mia.

Uncle Charlie, Danny and Eric all took turns looking through the periscope. There was a long thick rope stuck to the bottom of the skylab with a sucker. And climbing up the rope, with her catapult between her teeth, was Roxie.

Less than a minute later, the hatch in the middle of the floor swung open and Roxie clambered on board. Everyone hugged each other and laughed. Then Uncle Charlie told Roxie what had happened in the last couple of hours.

"So now he's got the amulet," said Roxie. "It's funny cos Jasper said that the Space Twister might be closing in on it. Said someone had been in Thelonius Grebe's old house before us. Oh well. We'd better get the amulet back, then."

"Where is Jasper?" asked Eric.

"Mr Jasper Gibbons stayed in Hamburg," said Roxie. "See, I spent an hour in Grebe's old study going through his journals, but a lot of them were in Latin. Jasper speaks the lingo so he stayed behind to find out how the amulet actually works. How DID I get to Hamburg by the way?"

Danny quickly explained how Eric had hacked the Time Tablet.

"Well, Agent Taylor!" exclaimed Roxie, ruffling Eric's hair. "I'm glad you're on our side."

"How did you get up here?" asked Mia.

"Well, Grebe had loads of rope hanging around," said Roxie. "He was always building pulleys and winches and stuff. And the sight on my catapult has a range of ten miles. So I just tied a plastic arrow with a sucker on to a length of rope and then knotted lots of rope together. Then I held on to the other end – and fired."

She smiled at everyone.

"So now we're all up to date," she said, "will someone please tell me what the plan is?"

"You said that when Roxie got here, I could go to the Science Palace," whined Eric.

"Yeah, well, I'm not so sure now," said Uncle Charlie. "It's all starting to feel dangerous again."

"Uncle, if you've thought of a way of getting my remote back, you should say," said Danny.

"If you know how to end this, so I can enjoy

the rest of my birthday on Planet Earth, spit it out," said Mia.

"All right, all right," said Uncle Charlie. "But you all have to promise to do EXACTLY as I say, OK?"

"OK," said Danny and Mia.

"Metal Gretel, here I come!" said Eric.

14
SCROLL DOWN

The skylab rode a strong thermal current upwards and then drifted west across the North Sea.

"We'll be in position in about three minutes. Everyone ready?" asked Uncle Charlie.

Danny, Eric and Mia nodded.

"I was born ready," said Roxie, tucking her catapult into her skirt.

"Tacking south," said Uncle Charlie. There was an instrument panel above his workbench. He pulled a small grey level and the balloon swerved left.

"OK," he continued. "Remember the plan. Me and Roxie will be out of range of the remote. So we'll also be missing from the Time Tablet.

But we'll be there. Watching your back."

He pulled another grey lever and the balloon slowed to a stop.

"You're now above Kensington," he said. "Just press this blue button to descend. Red button to ascend. No time to say anything but good luck. So: good luck."

Charlie opened the hatch in the middle of the skylab. Roxie jumped on his back. "I believe in you," he said. "All three of you."

Then he dropped through the hatch. Danny, Mia and Eric ran across to the window and watched Uncle Charlie and Roxie vanish into a cloud below.

Danny stared at the cloud for a couple of

minutes. Then he heard a clunking noise behind him and saw Mia standing by the instrument panel. "Ready?" she said.

Without waiting for a reply from Danny or Eric, she jammed her thumb down on the large blue button. The balloon started to sink directly downwards. Eric staggered sideways and knocked over a chair which hit a set of shelves which fell on a toolbox which landed on Mia's foot.

"Ow!" howled Mia.

"Sorry," said Eric, trying to stand up and knocking over another chair which hit a stack of paper which knocked over a monitor which landed on Mia's other foot.

"You idiot!" yelled Mia.

Well, this is a good start, thought Danny.

The balloon kept dropping like a lift, getting slowly faster. They passed quickly through the clouds and out the other side. Now they could see birds, and now distant hills and mountains. A few seconds later, London was sprawling out beneath them on every side.

Danny felt his Time Tablet beep and come back to life. "Time to put the brakes on," he shouted.

Mia pressed the red button and the balloon slowed down. At the point when it was starting to take off again, Mia pressed the blue button. When it picked up too much speed, she pressed the red button.

Eric and Danny stared out of the window, watching West London rise to meet them. They saw the top of the Space Twister's glass dome, then queues of people snaking away from the entrance doors.

Mia kept pressing the red button, then the blue button, letting them down gently.

The balloon stopped suddenly and swung Danny, Eric and Mia into each other and then on to the floor.

"Is that it?" said Eric, scrambling to his feet. "Are we here?"

Danny twisted his neck round and looked out of the window. "We appear to be stuck in a tree," he said.

"Brilliant," said Eric. "Nice one, Mia."

Mia looked at the leaves and branches that were squashed up against the windows. "If you hadn't broken both of my feet, then maybe I could have concentrated for longer," she hissed.

"Look, it's fine, it's fine," said Danny. "We're in the park behind the museum. Let's just drop through the hatch and go."

Mia narrowed her eyes at Eric and Eric stuck his tongue out at Mia.

Danny opened the hatch and said, "It's only a couple of metres down. Come on."

Mia and Eric peered over Danny's shoulder. "It looks a bit further than that," she said dubiously.

Then the balloon started to pull itself free of the tree.

"What the—" stammered Mia.

"Is it giving way?" said Eric.

"No, I don't think it's that," said Danny. "Come on, we've got to go."

The balloon started to rise.

"He's pressing Rewind," said Danny. "He's

seen the balloon, he's suspicious. Jump!"

Danny dropped through the hatch.

The balloon was now completely free of the branches. Mia looked through the hatch, gritted her teeth and jumped.

The balloon was rising faster, going backwards, up into the sky.

"Come on, jump!" called Danny and Mia from the ground, looking at Eric's face in the hatch as the balloon got further and further away.

"We'll catch you," said Danny. "Jump!"

"I can't believe I'm doing this," said Eric and dropped through the air, one metre, two metres, three, four, five, and then *whoomf* into Danny and Mia's arms.

They all stood up and were about to start arguing with each other, when they were struck dumb by what they saw. The balloon was a dot in the sky now. In front of them, people were sprinting backwards across the grass. Behind them, cars and buses were reversing back down the street.

"So this is what rewind looks like," Mia murmured.

"This is it," said Danny.

Everybody stopped and started going forward again. Buses roared past and taxis honked their horns.

"I'm glad the crystals work," said Eric, putting his tongue in one of his molars.

"My teeth are tingling," said Mia. "It's like I've just eaten too much ice cream."

Danny also felt for the crystal in one of his back teeth.

"OK, let's check out your Time Tablet," said Mia. "Remember what Uncle Charlie said before we left. The Time Tablet is our eyes and ears."

"Can't we just go?" asked Eric. "Look at it! I can see the top of Metal Gretel! I can see a lunar module!"

Danny was looking at his Time Tablet. He had typed in "Science Palace, Kensington". When it appeared, he clicked to look inside. There were thousands of folders.

"Look at this," Danny murmured. "Look at the names."

Mia looked over his shoulder and read the first twenty-eight names:

Andrew Jenkins	**Eric Booth**
Bernard Cranham	**Eric Bose**
Eric Adams	**Eric Burns**
Eric Akabusi	**Eric Burton**
Eric Allen	**Eric Butler**
Eric Anand	**Eric Chapman**
Eric Andrews	**Eric Chauhan**
Eric Armstrong	**Eric Chen**
Eric Atkins	**Eric Cheng**
Eric Baker	**Eric Chiang**
Eric Ball	**Eric Chopra**
Eric Banerjee	**Eric Clark**
Eric Barker	**Eric Clarke**
Eric Bell	**Eric Cole**

"I thought I might be able to find the Space Twister in here and just cut and paste him," said Danny, "but there's no chance. And look at all these Erics – I mean – it's too creepy—"

"Yeah," said Mia. "I reckon if Eric doesn't want to go ahead with this, then – Eric? Eric?"

They looked up and saw Eric in the distance, heading for a big door marked:

ENTRANCE FOR ERICS

"That's all we need," said Danny. "Come on, we've got to stick together or Uncle Charlie can't keep track of us."

Mia looked up at the sky. "You sure he can see us from up there?"

"Roxie's catapult has a range of ten miles," said Danny, "and the bank of clouds they're riding is only nine miles up."

They ran across the grass and caught up with Eric just as he was going through the door into the Science Palace.

"Eric, wait for us," said Danny.

But Eric was already approaching the bag-checking area. One thug stood next to a conveyor belt, staring at an X-ray screen. Another thug stood next to a big black security gate that beeped every time anyone walked through it.

Eric approached the gate. "I don't have anything metallic on me," he said.

"It's not a metal detector," the thug grunted. "It's an Eric detector. It sets off an alarm if your name's not Eric. Walk through slowly, stop in the middle, then carry on."

"Oh, OK," said Eric.

"Eric, we've got to stick to the plan," hissed Danny, taking a step forward.

But Mia held him back. "Don't draw attention to yourself," she whispered.

Eric walked into the gate, and a beam of red light passed down over his body then back up again. There was a high-pitched beep and a green light flashed above his head.

"Now come over here," said the thug on the gate. He was holding a hand stamp. "This is so you can go out and come back in again."

"It's OK," said Eric. "When I leave, I won't come back."

"You still have to have it," said the thug sternly, grabbing Eric's hand and pushing the hand stamp down sharply.

Eric felt a tiny pin-prick of pain. "Ow," he said, and yanked his arm back.

He looked down at his
hand and saw that a capital
E had been stamped in
blue ink in the middle of
his palm. Underneath it, a
drop of blood was trickling
on to his wrist.

"Enjoy your day of wonder
and discovery," grunted the thug, shoving Eric
through another door and into the Science
Palace itself.

Danny and Mia were still hovering on the
other side of the security gate.

"Did you see that?" said Mia.

The thug on the gate was staring at them.

"Are you Erics or aren't you?" he barked.

"Yes, I mean, no, I mean, yes," said Danny.

The thug narrowed his eyes and pulled a
photo out of his inside pocket. "Daniel and
Mia Danger," he muttered to himself. Then he
looked back up at Danny and Mia. But Danny
and Mia had gone.

They had run anti-clockwise around the glass

dome and were hiding behind a small electricity generator.

"OK, we have to get in there," said Danny. "That hand stamp was bizarre. Eric's in trouble."

"Totally, but how do we do it?" said Mia. "We can't go through the main entrance. They're clearly looking out for us. That thug had our photo."

"And I can't cut and paste us, because we're wearing crystals in our teeth. We're outside of time," said Danny.

Mia thought for a second. "We'll have to use my Mirror Key," she said firmly.

"But Uncle Charlie said we shouldn't," said Danny, "or he'll lose sight of us. And he won't know which mirror we're coming out of."

"Fine. Just let me know when you have a better idea," said Mia.

Danny thought for a few seconds – he could edit some Erics, or cut and paste some thugs – but that would cause confusion and alarm. Sneaking in through a mirror did make sense.

"Over here, Danny," whispered Mia, pointing at a shiny metal plaque on the side of the Science Palace. It read:

THIS DOME WAS OPENED BY
THE SPACE TWISTER, 2012

Mia was holding her key up to the surface. She moved it left and right until a keyhole appeared. She unlocked it and Danny and Mia crawled through.

"Nice to see you again," said Umberto cheerfully. "Been keeping busy?"

Mia asked Umberto for a list of all the mirrors in the Science Palace. There were hundreds to choose from. She chose one in the projection room of the IMAX cinema.

The mirror whirred into its new shape and Danny and Mia stepped through. They found themselves in a small dark room with a large box-shaped camera at one end. A middle-aged man was leaning on it, asleep.

Danny and Mia sneaked past the man and opened a soundproof door that led to a flight of stairs. They went down the stairs and emerged into the foyer of the IMAX cinema.

They were people everywhere, most of them boys between seven and eleven.

"Look at their hands," whispered Mia.

Most of the boys had a big blue E stamped on their right palms.

But Danny was staring past the cinema foyer and looking at everything else that had been squashed into the dome. He had a dreamy expression on his face. There were rockets and rides and slides and trains and giant TV screens and enormous telescopes and huge computers. Dominating it all was a massive steel robot with GRETEL spelled out on its back in flashing red lights and four rows of buttons on its chest.

Suddenly he felt a sharp elbow in his ribs. "This is no time to be a geek," said Mia. "We've got to find Eric."

Danny blinked and looked at his sister. "Oh, yeah. *Yeah.*"

"Let's stick to the edge of the dome," said Mia. "Out of sight when we can."

Danny was still half looking at all of the machines and gadgets and, above all, Metel Gretel. Mia yanked him behind a glass cabinet full of computers from the 1970s.

"Hello," said a deep voice and both Danny and Mia spun round.

"Hello," said another deep voice.

Two thugs had appeared, as if from nowhere.

"Hello," said a third thug and, "Look who it is," said a fourth.

Danny and Mia had their backs against the glass cabinet. Danny, terrified, managed to pull out his Time Tablet, but who should he search for? What should he type?

One of the thugs snatched the Time Tablet out of Danny's hands.

"This is no time to surf the bleedin' Internet, sunshine," said the thug. Danny recognised him as Barry, one of the bodyguards from

Grapeshot Hall.

"What did the boss say?" said a second thug. "Kill the girl but not the boy."

"Kill the girl and hurt the boy," said Barry. "We are allowed to hurt him."

"Can I do the killing? Please?" asked the second thug.

"That's not fair," said the third thug. "He always does the killing."

A tear was trickling out of Mia's eye. Danny was rigid with fear, unable to look at anything but the ground.

"Tough," said the second thug, lifting up his huge hand and holding it above Mia's head.

At that moment, the glass above them tinkled and a pellet whipped through the air and hit the second thug on the back of the head.

"Ow," he said. "That really hurt." Then his eyes rolled back in his head and he collapsed on the floor.

The thugs twisted round and looked up at the roof of the glass dome. Another pellet whipped through the air and hit Barry on the forehead.

He went cross-eyed and then slumped to the floor next to the second thug.

Danny grabbed his Time Tablet from Barry. Then both Danny and Mia ran away as fast as they could, more pellets raining down behind them.

15
SHUT DOWN

Danny and Mia sprinted towards the centre of the dome, where people were gathering around a spacewalk suit and a moon buggy.

"Thank goodness for Roxie," said Mia, still sniffling slightly. "She must have spotted us."

"No more using mirrors," said Danny. "We have to stay where Uncle Charlie and Roxie can see us."

Danny looked up. He imagined Roxie holding up her catapult and peering down the sight on the left prong. She and Uncle Charlie would be swinging backwards and forwards on the clouds, directly above their heads.

"Trouble is," said Danny, "the Space Twister must know we're here now."

"Yeah," said Mia, "and he might have realised that Roxie and Uncle Charlie are up there, ready to knock him out with a pellet."

"So maybe he won't show his face, after all," said Danny.

Then everyone in the Science Palace stopped moving. All of the rides went dead, all of the gadgets stopped flashing, the images on all of the screens froze. The world had been paused. The crystals in Danny and Mia's teeth started to tingle again.

The Space Twister walked calmly through the crowd, holding the remote in one hand and a gun in the other. When he reached the spot where Danny and Mia were standing, he said, "Wherever did you learn that trick with the amber crystals?"

The Space Twister was wearing a cape with a heavy hood. His face was hidden.

"Now don't move, or talk, or hit me with a pellet," said the Space Twister, "or this gun might accidentally go off."

He looked up, glancing through the glass

roof, then looked back down again.

Then he pulled back his hood.

Both Danny and Mia gasped. He was one of the oldest men that they had ever seen. His face was nothing but folds of wrinkled skin, hanging loosely from his skull. His eyes were tiny and bloodshot. Dark brown splotches covered his cheeks and neck. Thick black veins stuck out from his temples.

He put the remote in his pocket with a claw-like hand and pulled out a gold necklace.

"Grebe's amulet," said the Space Twister. "Activated at last. Put it on for me, Danny. My hands are shaky and I can't undo the clasp."

"What do you m-mean?" stammered Danny.

"Come on, help me put it on," said the Space Twister. "You're probably the only person on Earth who understands. It's the remote, isn't it, Danny? It's the remote's fault. Now put the amulet round my neck. You never know, I might let your sister live."

"You – you better let her live," said Danny, feeling suddenly angry, "and my friend Eric too."

"Ah, Eric," said the Space Twister. "That, I'm afraid, will be impossible. Now the amulet."

Danny hesitated, looking at his sister.

The Space Twister fired the gun, hitting the ground just in front of Mia.

"The amulet!" he squealed with a shrill, cracked voice.

"OK, OK," said Danny.

"Now!" screamed the Space Twister, firing again, narrowly missing Mia's leg. "Now! Now! Now!"

He fired repeatedly, the last bullet ripping a tear through Mia's sleeve.

As the Space Twister prepared to fire again, Eric leapt out from behind the moon buggy and squirted Truth Spray into the Space Twister's face.

"Tell us your darkest secret!" he shouted.

"What? What?" stammered the Space Twister. "What's going on?" Then his face went slack and he spoke quickly and evenly, "When I was a boy, I once stole fifty pounds from my father's wallet. You see, I wanted this model aeroplane and he said we couldn't afford it. Well, I wasn't about to take no for an answer so I took the money and headed to the toyshop as quickly as I could…"

A split second later, a pellet whipped through the glass roof and hit the Space Twister on the shoulder, sending him sprawling forward on to his face. The gun clattered on to the floor and spun away.

Eric, Mia and Danny hugged each other.

"Mia, Mia, are – are you OK?" gabbled Danny. "Did the bullets hit you?"

"Just my top," said Mia, "but you can buy me a new one for my birthday."

"We got him!" said Eric. "We totally got him. The plan worked."

"It nearly didn't!" cried Mia. "Because of you running off!"

The Space Twister was groaning and fiddling with something in his pocket.

"Is he still conscious?" asked Mia, frowning and looking over Danny's shoulder.

"You'd better grab the remote and that

amulet," said Eric.

The world suddenly sprang back to life. The Space Twister had pressed Play on the remote. Within a few seconds, dozens of people were crowding round the Space Twister, saying: "Are you OK, sir? What happened, sir?"

"Oh no!" exclaimed Danny, trying to fight his way through the crowd.

He heard more voices. "Are you all right, sir? Can I help you with that, sir?"

Eric appeared next to Danny, trying to push a short man with a large beard to one side.

The man with the beard said, "He's trying to tell us something. Let the old man speak."

Then a column of light flared up from where the Space Twister was lying. It shot through the glass dome and up into the sky. Everyone staggered back. The light got brighter and brighter and then collapsed in on itself and vanished.

Everyone was crouching down and covering their eyes.

A young man stepped forwards wearing

Grebe's amulet round his neck. He was perhaps twenty years old. He had one brown eye and one blue eye. He had black slicked-back hair and white unblemished skin. There was no scar cutting his face in two.

At the same moment, Eric turned pale and his legs gave way. The E on his right hand was no longer written in blue ink, but in dark red blood.

Two metres away, another boy fainted. He also had a scarlet E on his right hand.

Behind the moon buggy, two more boys passed out. In front of the giant TV, beside the huge robot, next to the fairground rides, more boys fell like dominos. They dropped on to their knees, drained of life.

Mothers and fathers screamed in terror.

Another pellet flew through the glass roof and hurtled towards the Space Twister. He glanced up and danced nimbly out of the way.

"Eric? Eric?" Danny was murmuring. "What's wrong? Eric?" He looked up and saw the Space Twister looking down at him. "What have you done to him?" he demanded. "What have you done?"

"Taken his youth," said the Space Twister. "If only you hadn't come today, he might still be alive."

Another pellet tore through the glass roof, but once more the Space Twister stepped lightly aside.

"They should be more careful," said the Space Twister. "That nearly hit your sister."

Mia was crouching down beside Danny, looking up at the Space Twister like a cat about to pounce.

"Now I'm in a quandary," said the Space Twister, leaning down to pick up his gun. "You see, if I kill you, the remote won't work. Because it thinks I'm you. But then, I don't really need the remote any more. Because time can't hurt me now. So, given that you and your friends keep trying to spoil my fun, I think I'll go for ... a dead remote and a dead Danny."

There was another tinkling sound overhead. The Space Twister looked up again, but this time the pellet was nowhere near him. Instead, it seemed to be flying towards Metal Gretel, the giant robot that was standing at the back of the glass dome.

The pellet hit a large red button on Metal Gretel's chest.

"So destroy the robot," hissed the Space Twister. "Like I care. Now, Danny..."

The red button turned green and Metal Gretel lifted up one of her giant legs, bringing it down with a heavy, hissing stamp.

There was even more screaming.

Metal Gretel swung her other leg forward, pulling down the wires and guy-ropes that were holding her in place.

The Space Twister looked around in fury and pulled a walkie-talkie out of a holster in his belt.

Metal Gretel took two more huge steps forward, making the ground shake as she stomped through glass cases and roped-off displays.

The Space Twister was shouting into the walkie-talkie. "Ronald! Barry! Get here now! Stop that robot! The children called Eric must not be harmed!"

Parents were trying to drag their unconscious children out of the way and towards the exit.

Metal Gretel flung her left arm out sideways and bashed a hole in the glass dome. Then she took another step forward and squashed a hover-scooter.

Danny and Mia had dragged Eric behind a giant satellite dish that shielded them from view.

Danny was switching on his Time Tablet.

"He's still breathing," said Mia, putting her hand on Eric's chest.

"Right, take the crystal out of his mouth," said Danny, "so he appears in the Time Tablet."

Mia rooted around in Eric's teeth and extracted the crystal. "Yuk," she said.

Danny typed Eric Taylor into the Time Tablet and Eric's file flashed up on the screen. Danny clicked into it and typed:

Eric opened his eyes and stood up.

But the sentence vanished and changed to:

Eric tried to wake up, but he couldn't.

Danny typed:

Eric summoned up all his strength and opened his eyes.

The sentence changed to:

Eric was in a coma and couldn't wake up, no matter how much he tried.

"Drat!" exclaimed Danny. "It must be physically impossible."

In front of the satellite dish, there was more smashing and screaming as Metal Gretel crunched her way through the Science Palace.

"It's linked to the Space Twister," said Mia. "When he put the amulet on, all the children called Eric collapsed. They all had an E on their hands."

Danny started typing into the Time Tablet. "The Space Twister told me that he'd stolen Eric's youth," he said. "He must have done the same to every Eric in the building."

"OK, so what are you doing?" asked Mia.

"The Space Twister must be in here somewhere," said Danny. "He's not wearing a crystal. I'm going to find him and delete him. Delete him forever."

"Wait, wait," said Mia. "If you delete him, you might delete Eric too. Say the Space Twister really has stolen Eric's youth? Then they're sort of one person. We have to work out exactly what the Space Twister has done before we delete him."

Then time stopped and all was still. The Space Twister had pressed Pause on the remote.

"Get out here! Both of you! Now!" shouted the Space Twister, his voice echoing in the silent glass cavern.

"Look, I'll distract him," said Mia. "You find

out what his powers are and how we can beat him."

"OK, but—" started Danny.

"It's the only way," said Mia. "Look, did you see behind those fairground rides? There was a hall of mirrors. I should be able to keep him busy in there for a few minutes."

She turned round and ran along the side of the dome. She found a solar panel with a mirrored surface, unlocked it and jumped in. Before she vanished, she shouted, "Oi, scarface. Over here."

The Space Twister ran towards the sound.

Danny stared at his Time Tablet and tried to think. He looked down at Eric and tried to think. He thumped his head with his hand, hoping to jolt his brain into action.

Without realising it, he had whispered, "Jasper."

Roxie had said that Jasper was staying behind in Hamburg to find out more about the amulet. Roxie had mentioned Jasper's surname too – what was it? GIBBONS popped into Danny's head.

Mia's voice was now coming from the other side of the dome. "Come and get me!" she shouted.

Danny poked his head up from behind the satellite dish and tried to work out where Mia was. Behind Metal Gretel, he could see the edge of the hall of the mirrors. Mia's head was sticking out of a convex mirror near the entrance. The Space Twister was running towards it, shouting: "Get out here and fight!"

Danny sat back down again and read the end of Jasper's file:

Jasper opened the book and saw Grebe's famous riddle on the first page. The first two lines Jasper already knew: "My face is gold, my case is gold/For gold keeps out the wind and cold." But the last four were new to him:

"And if you take the prize from me
From Father Time, you will be free.
If ten score drops of blood you drain
From youths who share your Christian name."

Jasper looked at the diagram of the amulet

underneath the riddle. It had an opening at the top a few millimetres wide. The inside appeared to be hollow. The two circles of gold that formed the amulet were only half a centimetre thick. It looked like it was designed to contain something – something liquid. Reading the poem again, Jasper could only conclude that it was meant to contain blood.

But blood from where? Ten score drops – that was two hundred drops of blood. From young people that share your name? How could you possibly persuade children to give you their blood?

Jasper turned the page and saw another drawing in Grebe's journal. It showed a human wearing the amulet, restored to his youthful self. Around him, there were sketches of sleeping children. There was a Latin phrase underneath the diagram that Jasper translated into English. "To wake the children, pour out the blood."

Danny heard more glass breaking and Mia shouting: "Better luck next time!"

He thought back over the past hour. The Space Twister had taken the amulet but it wasn't going to work unless he filled it with two hundred drops of blood from children with the same Christian name as him. Eric. The Space Twister's first name must be Eric.

The Science Palace was just a way of luring children called Eric to one place. The hand stamp on the way in had taken a drop of blood from each child. When the Space Twister had taken enough blood, he'd filled the amulet with it. And when he'd put the amulet on, every Eric in the Science Palace had collapsed.

Danny needed to think faster than ever. "To wake the children, pour out the blood." So first of all, he needed to get the amulet from around the Space Twister's neck.

He took the crystal out of his teeth so that he would appear in the Time Tablet. Then he typed in his own name.

"Only one mirror left," yelled the Space Twister from the other side of the dome. "It's time to show yourself."

Danny found his own file and chose Edit. After the last sentence, he typed: "The Space Twister walked across the Science Palace and handed Danny the amulet."

The sentence changed to: "The Space Twister thought about handing Danny the amulet but decided to keep it."

It's no good, Danny thought, *I need to find his file. I need to get inside his mind.* Then a thought flashed into Danny's head and he typed in "Science Palace, Kensington".

He knew the Space Twister's first name. Eric.

The Science Palace appeared and Danny clicked inside. There were about fifty people who were still in the glass dome: just over forty of them were Erics.

Danny scanned the small photos that sat on top of each folder.

"Mr Danger!" declared the Space Twister suddenly. "I've got your sister! Come out from your hiding place or I'll blow her brains out."

There was the Space Twister's picture. There was his folder. Eric Davidson.

"You're the one whose head is about to explode!" shouted Danny, stepping out from behind the satellite dish with the Time Tablet in his hand.

He looked around at the Science Palace. Metal Gretel was frozen mid-step. There were still dozens of people as stiff as statues, stopped dead on their way to the exit. Over by the hall of mirrors, there was broken glass everywhere.

"You and your sister are about to be ejected from time," said the Space Twister, walking towards Danny. Mia was next to him, with a gun wedged in her side.

Danny clicked on the Space Twister's folder and selected Cut. The Space Twister vanished.

Danny navigated to Brazil on the world map and pasted the Space Twister into the middle of the Amazon jungle. He clicked Cut again, then he found the La Brea Tar Pits in Los Angeles and clicked Paste. He dropped the Space Twister in the Grand Canyon and the Paris sewage system and the middle of the M1 motorway and the top of the Greenland ice sheet and the Kruger National Park and finally, when he was covered with filth and sunburnt and frostbitten and half-eaten by lions, the

Space Twister was duly pasted back into the Science Palace.

He was a crumpled heap on the floor. Danny walked across to him and pulled down the collar of his jacket. He grabbed the amulet and yanked it over the Space Twister's head.

A column of red light shot out of the Space's Twister's back, lifted him half a metre off the ground and slowly faded, dropping him gently back down again.

Mia had appeared next to Danny. "I turned off Metal Gretel and tied up the thugs," she said. "What have we got here?" She turned the Space Twister over with her foot.

He was an old man again. He looked frailer than ever, barely able to open his eyes or move his lips. He was clutching the remote in one of his gnarled, shrivelled hands.

Danny prized the remote out of the Space Twister's fist.

He felt the amber crystal glowing in his hand and felt immediately calm.

"Let's try and put things back to normal,"

said Danny.

He pressed Play and the Science Palace was a blaze of noise and activity again.

"We need to wake up the Erics," said Mia.

Danny nodded and put the remote in his front pocket.

"If I pour the blood out of the amulet, the Erics should go back to normal," said Danny.

The Space Twister started to giggle. "The old gadgets are the best," he said.

Mia and Danny looked down and saw that the Space Twister had a gun in his hand. He aimed at Mia's chest and fired.

Danny thought, *It's point blank range. Mia's dead. Mia's been killed.*

He thought, *I've got no time to get the remote out of my pocket.*

He thought, *Grace Bingley's nickname was the Bullet. She twisted space and slowed down time.*

Danny focused on the noise of the gun firing. He slowed down the sound and felt it getting lower and longer and deeper. He concentrated harder until the gunshot was hardly a noise at all, just a dim, deep rumble. At the same time, he threw himself sideways, between the Space Twister and Mia.

He noticed that the Space Twister had frozen, a triumphant grin on his face.

The world was almost silent now. There was a faint buzzing noise in his ears, that was all.

At the same time, he felt a burning sensation in his chest. As he tumbled sideways, it became sharper, cutting across his face and ripping through his body. He could feel time pressing on him, desperate to move, determined to resist any efforts to twist or stop or alter it.

Danny could see almost nothing now. Mia and the Space Twister were just blurred outlines.

Then it was as if he was torn in half. He felt the two parts of his body hit the floor with a thump.

When he woke up, Mia, Eric, Uncle Charlie, Roxie and Jasper were all standing round him. He looked up at the glass roof of the Science Palace.

"Will he be scarred for life?" asked Mia.

"No," said Uncle Charlie. "He pulled back in time. It'll take a while for the cut to heal, though."

"Does it go all the way down his body like the Space Twister's?" asked Eric.

Uncle Charlie nodded and then noticed that Danny was awake. "Hey, nephew," he said. He frowned. "Listen, you've got to promise never to try that again. Ever. It might not hurt a space twister like Grace Bingley. But for normal people like me and you … it kills."

"I promise," whispered Danny. "I really, really do."

"Good," said Uncle Charlie. "Because we all

need you here."

Danny nodded and said, "How did you get down from the clouds so quickly?"

"You've been out for twenty minutes," said Mia.

"We started to fly down just after we switched on the giant robot," said Uncle Charlie.

"Yeah, sorry, ran out of pellets towards the end," said Roxie. "That's why we stopped firing at the Space Twister."

"It's OK," said Danny, looking up dreamily. "It all worked out OK."

He put his left hand to his face and felt the line of dry blood that ran along his nose, down his chin and on to his neck.

"I thought you'd been shot," said Mia, looking at Danny with a smile.

"I thought you'd been shot," Danny replied.

He opened his right hand and held it up. A single bullet was sitting in the middle of his palm.

"Nice catch, Danny," he said to himself.

They talked for the next fifteen minutes, everyone explaining what they had seen and done.

Mia said she had tipped the blood out of the amulet to wake up all the Erics. Eric said he had found Grebe's golden eagle in a cage by the staff entrance.

Behind them, Jasper was using direct matter transfer to empty the glass dome, returning some objects to their original owners, moving other objects to nearby museums, disassembling others and placing them in boxes and crates. A vertical drop ride hovered in mid-air for a few minutes and was then placed neatly alongside a row of virtual reality simulators.

"Can we go home now?" asked Eric. "Being in a coma is exhausting."

"Sure," said Uncle Charlie. "We can ask Jasper to move us with his mind, if you like. Or I can take you by sky rope. Or we can use Mia's Mirror Key."

"Or Danny can cut and paste us," Eric added. "Don't forget that."

"Of course!" exclaimed Uncle Charlie. "I haven't tried it yet. Fun, is it?"

"It's like having your brain sucked out of your ear and then injected back in through your nose," said Eric. "It's brilliant!"

Danny listened to them talk and gave a half-smile. Mia noticed and said, "Ready to help me celebrate my birthday?" she asked.

"Yeah," said Danny. "Can't wait to get back to Mum and Dad. Non-stop fun."

Jasper appeared next to Mia and said, "Finished!"

"Is everything back in its rightful place?" Uncle Charlie asked him.

"More or less," said Jasper. "I moved the golden eagle to Ben Nevis rather than Everest. So we can keep an eye on him. And I kept one or two gadgets for research purposes obviously. They're in the EUREKA! HQ."

"But we don't have an HQ at the moment," said Uncle Charlie.

"I know," said Jasper. "I set up a new temporary HQ."

"Where?" asked Uncle Charlie.

"Well, I tried to pick somewhere unlikely," said Jasper, "somewhere that looked nothing like our previous HQs. So I went for ... er ... Danny's bedroom."

Danny's mouth dropped open.

"You did what?" exclaimed Uncle Charlie.

"But hang on," said Danny, "my room's full of rubbish. Mum and Dad filled it with bin liners."

"Oh yes, those," said Jasper. "Obviously I had to move them first."

"Where to?" asked Danny.

"Well, ahem, I put them in your parents' room," said Jasper.

Danny and Mia both looked shocked. Then they grinned at each other.

"Is that a problem?" asked Jasper.

"Nope," answered Danny and Mia together.

They all headed out of the glass dome.

"What happened to the Space Twister?" asked Danny.

"You can read the full story in your Time

Tablet," said Uncle Charlie. "You'll find his file in the Happy Valley Twilight Home for the Criminally Insane."

They walked through the doors of the Science Palace and out into the evening sunshine.

Danny turned to Mia and said, "You know what? Maybe we shouldn't go home yet. It *is* your birthday, after all."

"What do you mean?" asked Mia.

"I mean, shouldn't we have a party?" said Danny.

Eric was just behind Danny and Mia. "Did someone just say party?" he asked.

"I suppose a party would be nice," said Mia, "but where shall we have it?"

"Anywhere you like," said Danny. "Hawksby Caves? Grapeshot Hall? Mount Everest?"

Mia thought for a moment. "How about the skylab? That'd be out of this world."

Danny, Mia and Eric all looked up at the clouds.

"Last one there's a dork," said Danny.

Have you read Danny's first fantastic adventure?

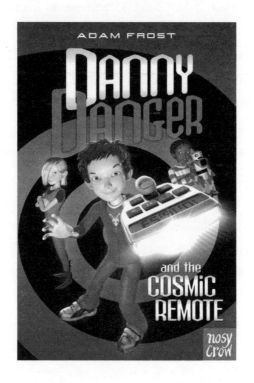

www.nosycrow.com